# EMMA'S CHRISTMAS ROSE

Apart from their inability to conceive a child, Emma and Paul Sykes are completely happy. Unexpectedly their housekeeper, Eileen, becomes pregnant and her soldier husband, Mick, vows to avoid the developing crisis in Korea. Still bitterly resentful that Emma has abandoned her to marry Paul, Emma's mother dies without making peace with her daughter and leaves her estate in the dubious hands of a stranger. Meanwhile, in her haven on the Isle of Wight, Emma's Aunt Emily cultivates a unique Christmas Rose, guaranteed to bloom at a time of bleak scarcity in gardens—a sign of hope and future promise ...

# EMMA'S CHRISTMAS ROSE

# EMMA'S CHRISTMAS ROSE

*by*
Elizabeth Daish

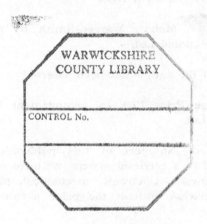
**Magna Large Print Books**
Long Preston, North Yorkshire,
England.

British Library Cataloguing in Publication Data.

---

Daish, Elizabeth
  Emma's Christmas Rose.

  A catalogue record for this book is
  available from the British Library

  ISBN 0-7505-1247-4


First published in Great Britain by Severn House Publishers
Ltd., 1997

Copyright © 1997 by Elizabeth Daish

Cover illustration © Melvyn Warren-Smith by arrangement
with P.W.A. International Ltd.

The moral right of the author has been asserted

Published in Large Print 1998 by arrangement with Severn
House Publishers Ltd.

Magna Large Print is an imprint of
Library Magna Books Ltd.
Printed and bound in Great Britain by
T.J. International Ltd., Cornwall, PL28 8RW.

*To Valerie*

# Chapter One

'When Mick came back to London the last time, he brought a few nice bits with him,' Eileen Grade said.

'Your husband is a miracle,' Emma Sykes laughed. 'He is far too honest to be a spiv and deal on the black market, but he seems able to get a lot more than the ordinary man in the street.'

'He seems to know a lot of what goes on before it happens,' Eileen said.

'Where is he now? I was too busy to see him go but he asked to borrow an overnight bag.'

'He's gone to see his old commanding officer for an ex-service get-together of men in his former unit. He has a place in Surrey, so we may get some rabbits.' Eileen sighed. 'We could all do with a change of diet. You haven't been to the Island lately, and we miss the nice things your aunt sends back with you.'

'You feed us very well, and I'm afraid you've had most of the cooking to do lately,' Emma said. She regarded her with affection and marvelled at the change in Eileen's looks and confidence since she and Mick moved in to the basement flat of the house in Kensington. The once pale and almost silent girl had blossomed, and she showed her gratitude for the comfortable, warm rooms and the easy atmosphere of the house and psychiatric clinic by working hard as the housekeeper, while Mick dealt with paperwork and the occasional session with unstable patients receiving treatment from Dr Paul Sykes, whose private practice had grown beyond his expectations.

'I've made a pot of tea. The last patient has gone and I took a cup to the doctor, but he said he'll stay in the office as he has a bit of bookwork to do.'

Emma sat down on the rather hard horsehair-stuffed settee inside the front hall and accepted her cup with a sigh of thanks. 'I can spare half an hour, but if I sit in a more comfortable chair I shall want to stay. How did I ever think I could have the time to go back to the Princess Beatrice to work after I was married?'

'You do quite enough here.' Eileen sounded like a fussy aunt. 'You work hard with Dr Paul and the patients love you. I know you enjoyed working at Beatties, but the last time you went there you said that all your old friends had left and there was only a sister in Casualty and the one in the private patients' wing that you really felt comfortable with.'

'It wasn't the same,' Emma admitted. 'I think I missed Bea more that day than I do here. Somehow this place will always have something of her and Dwight and the twins. She wrote last week and asked when we plan to go to Washington to see them, but we haven't had time to go to the Isle of Wight to see my Aunt Emily, let alone America.'

'Is her husband really out of the American air force now?' Eileen shook her head and smiled. 'He was a one! Made me laugh and teased the life out of me but never in a way to give offence.'

'He's on the reserve list and wears uniform on some occasions but is serving in the diplomatic corps close to the president, so they haven't managed to live on the Texas ranch where his family are. Bea is upset because the twins are growing fast and she thinks they need the country and ponies and more freedom, but she refuses to take them away from Dwight as his job is fairly difficult at times.'

'They can't be big enough to sit on horses, so what's the rush?'

'Bea thinks they should ride before they can walk, but they haven't managed to get the Shetland ponies that they want and there's plenty for them to do in Washington.'

'You'd think that everything would be sorted out by now. The Japs have been beaten and it's 1948 and peaceful. Not that I've noticed much difference except for no blackout and no bombs. Rationing is worse then ever and the last time I bought a blouse the seams fell apart after one wash.'

'I warned you against the spivs who sell out of suitcases in Oxford Street,' Emma pointed out mildly.

'You don't have to tell me! Mick was furious and said I must never buy from them again. One woman bought nylons all nicely wrapped up and found they had no feet when she got home! They sell and move on and you can never catch the blighters.'

'Sooner or later Paul will have to go to the States, as they've asked him to lecture on battle fatigue and the long-term effect of what they called shell shock in the First World War. We've had a lot of experience here and Paul has compiled a very impressive file on his treatment of bad cases, through hypnosis and analysis.'

'Mick and me will look after the place when you go,' Eileen said. 'At least I hope so.'

'Something wrong? You aren't thinking of leaving us?' Emma's alarm was real.

'No but he did say that there might be another war and if there was, he could be called up again.'

'But he's been demobbed as unfit for service after his accident and we are at peace with the Germans and the Japanese.'

'That's what I told him but you know Mick. He thinks a lot and reads the newspapers more than I do. He went to this get-together to see what's happening. He'll keep his ear to the ground and sum up the situation before he's told anything officially.'

A sudden sense of foreboding made Emma think of the last letter from Bea, the friend she'd had since they both started their nursing careers, first in Bristol and then at the Princess Beatrice Hospital in south-east London, and when Eileen went to answer the doorbell, Emma took her second cup of tea up to the office by the consulting room and sat with Paul while he made notes.

He smiled and saw that she was uneasy. 'What's up?'

'Could there be another war?'

'... Yes.'

'I thought we'd won!'

'It could blow up in the Far East.' His voice was mild, even casual, the voice that Emma had heard so many times when he wanted a patient to stay calm, and she eyed him with deep suspicion.

'All right,' he conceded. 'It could happen in Korea and soon, but it can't come here. No more bombs on London.'

'But we could go there? Eileen said that Mick hinted as much.'

'Ex-service officers and men could be called up under the blue flag of the United Nations as a strictly peacekeeping force but it's really an American affair. General MacArthur, the man who signed the peace with Japan and is now based in Tokyo, seems to think that the communists in North Korea are a great threat and that the division between North and South by the 38th parallel will be violated and a war might break out. Personally, I think he's a megalomaniac with a hatred of all creeds such as communism and he could land America into a lot of trouble. From what Dwight said in his letter, he hints that President Truman has doubts about MacArthur, too.'

'They couldn't take you?'

'I already do a lot of consultancy work for army personnel and they like me to be here.' Paul drew a squiggle on his blotter with a pencil that needed sharpening and the Mickey Mouse he'd attempted had no ears. 'However, Mick might not be so lucky and of course Dwight is American and was a famous pilot, now in the heart of Washington politics, so who knows what might happen there? He had a lot of flying experience and knows more about war than boys fresh from the academies, so he could be useful.' He hugged her and she relaxed. 'Don't worry about it. It might never happen.'

'I'll write to Bea tonight. If she hears rumours of war, she'll need to know we are still around.' She smiled more cheerfully. 'If Dwight went away, she might manage to come over to us for a while.'

'Not good.'

She looked up into his sombre face. 'But Paul, we've missed her and the twins. You sound as if you don't want her here!'

'Of course I do but I'm afraid for Dwight if he is entangled in war again.'

'He wouldn't be too vulnerable. With his rank and experience he would be a back-room boffin and probably not even fly a lot.'

'Let's hope that sanity prevails, but find out from Bea the names of Dwight's chiefs of staff who could make the suggestion that he goes to war. Dwight is a proud man and would go and take on what might not be good for him.'

'Why? What is worrying you?'

'Remember the time when I had to treat him for battle fatigue and he was impotent for a while, believing that he had personally dropped the bomb on Hiroshima?'

'Who could forget that! But it was long ago and he obviously recovered fully because the twins were born.'

'Have you heard of napalm?'

'No, is it some kind of a bomb again?'

'Not like that bomb, but deadly like an enormous chemical flame-thrower and the effects of it can be seen in all its horror afterwards. It's a firebomb that shoots across a wide target area, defoliating the trees and burning everything in its path: people, cattle and crops. The Americans have done exploratory tests of its capabilities and will use it in Korea if the rumours of war are true and its use isn't stopped by international law.'

Emma gasped. 'They would need observers in aircraft to photograph the napalm bombings and the damage, wouldn't they? People like Dwight who had that experience at Hiroshima? For Dwight it could be as he felt when *the* bomb was dropped.'

'Exactly. He must never go on such a mission.'

'What can we do? I feel so helpless with Bea and Dwight on the other side of the Atlantic.'

'It isn't certain that there will be a war, so try not to suffer in advance.' His smile was warm and reassuring and he held her close. 'I can say nothing until we hear if he is to be sent out east. However, when Bea makes her monthly phonecall, I'd like to speak to her instead of letting you two have all the time to yourselves. In your letter, ask for those names so that she can tell me when she rings, as I may be able to help in an emergency, if necessary without

Dwight knowing that I am doing so.'

'I see. You can say that you treated him privately for a psychiatric functional disorder related to battle fatigue and he might have a reaction to any similar situation that caused it? Is that what you mean? You are a genius.' Her eyes were wide and solemn. 'You had it in mind ages ago.'

'I have a full dossier in that drawer. If the balloon goes up and a crisis threatens and I am not available, you can send it by means of the Royal Air Force to Washington to the name that Bea must obtain for me, or Bea's father could arrange for it to be sent in the diplomatic bag to Washington. He has a lot of influence now in Parliament and would do anything to help his daughter and her husband. The details of Dwight's case this end are in the folder, and I think I'd like to talk to Bea about it, well before it happens. That is, if it does,' he added mildly. 'What a lot of worryguts we are about our friends.'

'Not that, just caring.'

Emma wrote her letter and sealed the envelope ready for posting to go by airmail, her one extravagance that didn't make her feel guilty. She glanced at the time and found it was early enough to send the letter that day so she told Paul that she was slipping out for ten minutes and hurried down the road to the new post office that had risen above the ashes of the old one bombed so long ago.

Other shops had appeared on the old bombed sites making living in the district much easier, and the whole area had an aura of recovery, by the side of the now carefully-kept park.

I must go over into the middle of the park and say hello to Peter Pan, she thought, but not today. The visit to the statue to eternal youth that Bea had loved so much would have to wait. Paul had a meeting at St Thomas's tonight and they must eat early.

She picked a dead leaf off the well-clipped bay tree by the right side of the front door. The other one on the left was immaculate and she must remember to send Bea another photograph of the two trees that had been gifts from Dwight to give the house a prosperous air when Paul was just starting his practice. She smiled. Not much wickedness in our house but the green bay tree flourishes. So much reminded her of them. The apartment that they'd used when the twins were born and afterwards until they went to America, was as it had been when they lived there, as if awaiting their return. The empty rectangular space left by the ancient four-poster bed bought in a house sale on the Isle of Wight and now sitting incongruously in a ranch house in Texas, was the only sign that they had gone.

There was a group of hopeful people outside the butcher's shop. It was not the shop where Emma and Eileen did their shopping for the meat ration, as some said the meat was rather tough horse, but sometimes he made sausages, the contents of which few people dared to guess, and liver sold there was safe and fresh from whichever animal it came. She stopped and the doors opened for custom. Almost by habit after seeing a line of people waiting for something that might be useful, Emma joined the others and found herself by a counter where a large white enamelled tray was piled high with chitterlings that glistened like pale snakes.

Although she and Paul never ate them, perhaps because they had memories of similar sights of guts in the operating theatres of the hospital, she knew that

Mick and Eileen liked them, so she bought what was allowed, two pounds in weight per person, a kind of rationing but providing far more protein than the conventional meat ration from the coupons in the ration books. Off-ration food was precious and she bought a pound of ox liver and some tripe.

She took her buys to the kitchen hastily as the wrapping paper was already leaking, and she had forgotten to take a sheet of newspaper in her holdall to use as an outer wrapping for anything likely to seep through the fragile paper. Would there ever be a time again when women not dressed up for a special date would not have to carry a holdall to take whatever came their way as extra rations or bargains?

Eileen was there, washing up Emma's tea tray and she gloated over the chitterlings. 'They'll be lovely with vinegar. Mick will be pleased,' she said. 'Sure you don't want any? I'll take them down to our kitchen—as they are so fresh we can have them tonight and tomorrow, and then there's no need to put them in your fridge.'

'Mick should be home soon, and you'll need some time together. I can cook our suppers as Paul has to go out later. That leaves you free for the rest of the day.'

Emma reconstituted dried milk, ready to make a white sauce for the tripe and sliced a couple of onions. Maybe not a true *'tripe a la mode de Caen'*, but it would do well with a bay leaf and mashed potatoes topped with scrapings of hard cheese.

Eileen lingered, ready to chat now that the bulk of work had been done. 'I made Mick take a hessian bag lined with oiled silk and some newspaper just in case he gets something from the country. He took his old army rucksack with his overnight things so he didn't need the bag you lent him. He thought it made him look like a civilian! I told him he is one now he's out of the army and made him wear his best demob suit. I hope he doesn't get interested in the army again.'

'I've been thinking about clothes,' Emma said. 'We need a few more hooks in the downstairs lobby for wet coats that patients want to leave before they go in to see Paul.' She frowned. 'I'll ask Mick to move that heavy umbrella stand out of sight. I like it in the hall as it's rather elegant but I have a feeling that someone took a rather nice walking stick.' She laughed. 'Some of our patients are habitual kleptomaniacs, so I shouldn't be surprised if they are tempted to do a little pilfering here.'

Mick returned with a couple of rabbits and a satisfied expression. 'They can hang for a day and I'll skin them tomorrow after they've been in the cold larder,' he said, walking briskly to the huge cool room that had once been the only means of keeping food fresh in the big house. Eileen went with him to their own flat and Emma tided up the consulting room and the downstairs lobby where the coats hung.

She stood by the umbrella stand, admiring the writhing dragon and the Chinese chrysanthemums carved into the wood. It was a lovely piece and a shame to hide it, but if someone had been light-fingered, it was silly to keep it on view. The shabby umbrellas were not pretty but very useful and the collection of walking sticks hid the faded silk covers. Her eye glanced at a particular one and she was puzzled. I could have sworn it had gone, she thought. I *know* it wasn't here last night. She picked up the smoothly-polished walking stick, spiralled like a barley sugar cane with a fox's-head handle and made by a farmer on the Isle of Wight, a treasured gift to Paul.

'Paul? Am I going mad?'

'Possibly, if you live here.'

'Your twisted stick vanished a couple of days ago and reappeared today.'

'Don't look at me. I may have cramp after sitting with patients all day but I don't need it yet.' He grinned. 'Ask Mick if he knows about it.'

'Mick? He left off using walking aids long ago. He has recovered completely from his broken legs.'

'When he was demobbed, he walked first with elbow crutches and then with sticks when his legs got tired, but I agree that he has no need of them now. He really worked at his recovery and exercised every day and now his legs are better than many that have never been injured.' Paul looked at her sideways. 'I think that if a man suffers injury and gets his army pension increased because of it, then recovers through his own efforts, refusing to sit on his backside grumbling about life, and gets on with a useful job of work, he is entitled to keep his benefit. It never wipes out his injury and suffering. Not a good opinion for a doctor to give but fortunately I am not his GP or his army doctor, and Mick certainly doesn't need me as a shrink! If he'd had a few more educational advantages in his early life, he'd have been very successful now.'

'He hasn't done badly. He was a sergeant and men respected him. When Bea and I knew him in hospital, he was wonderful. From his wheelchair he helped us with notes and bookwork and chivvied the men to make dressings and keep the ward tidy, and still kept his humour intact.' She eyed her husband accusingly. 'What do you know that I don't, among a hundred other things?'

'I saw him with my curly stick, trying it for size.'

'Why?'

'Maybe he took it into the country,' was all that he would say, and turned back to his ledger.

Emma regarded his head bent industriously over his work. Her face held an amused smile. 'Mick brought us some rabbits. Someone on the estate shot them so he didn't need a big stick to bash them with. Maybe someone, in his own good time, will tell me what's going on around here?'

Paul closed the book and laughed. 'I'm as intrigued as you are. Mick went off as if returning to his unit after leave, the perfect willing little soldier with brightly polished shoes and a clean shirt and the air of one who obeys his commanding officer in all things.'

Emma was aghast. 'Does that mean he wants to go back into the army? I thought he was happy here. What would Eileen do without him now? They are really happy.'

'I think it means just the opposite. Mick will not go back unless he is forced to do so, but can't you imagine him greeting old friends and talking of old times as if he really missed it all? His old CO would watch everything they did during that visit.'

She looked puzzled. 'But you said he doesn't want to go back.'

'Take that picture further. One very noticeable large walking stick, ornate enough to invite comment which he would shrug away with a brave grin as a bit of affectation, a little window dressing that he liked to have with him but didn't need, but as he asked, yes, his legs had been badly broken and given him a lot of trouble, but it was nothing, really nothing, and now he could do anything that any other man could do.' Paul gave her a shrewd look.

'As a nursing sister,' she began slowly.

'Go on, what would you think if a patient presented himself to you with that holy self-deprecating attitude about his medical condition?'

'I'd think he was being brave and a bit foolish to try to convince me that he was able to do far more than was physically possible, just to get back to work or on duty before he was ready.' She giggled. 'He hasn't changed. He was always a devious old devil in hospital. He could get us supplies that we had signed for and never had delivered and he was good with the men and helped them with discharge papers and pension rights. He got supplies and nobody really knew how he did it, but he didn't do it by lying. He should have been a lawyer, but he said he was too honest for that!'

'He would have no need to lie about this, either. He would make other people jump to the conclusions he wanted them to think and just nod and smile but say nothing against what they had convinced themselves was the correct answer.' He grinned. 'That particular stick was a masterly stroke. It

29

would show silently and rather poignantly that he needed it, but hoped he could fool himself and others that it was just a bit of lovely wood he enjoyed having with him, just as a Regency buck carried a gold-headed cane to add to his image.'

'You knew he had taken it?'

'Yes. What's he doing now?'

'Probably eating chitterlings with vinegar.'

Paul shuddered. 'Rather him than me.'

'He has to keep up his strength if he goes back into the army, but he is so fit that surely nobody would believe that he couldn't cope with a third world war if necessary?'

'I follow the mental processes of that man with awed interest, and as for his practical abilities, he has good ideas.' He led her to the consulting room. 'Look at this.'

'It's a bedside light switch. You don't need one in here as you have a reading lamp away from the patient and they are always more comfortable in dim light. Where is the light for this? I suppose he hasn't finished connecting it.' Emma looked at the bare wall behind the couch where there was no fresh light fitting and held the small bulb-like piece of Bakelite which hung on a wire under the couch. She pressed the small red button. A loud bell sounded in the office, the sound penetrating the far corners of the house and Paul ran to turn it off.

'You OK up there?' Mick called.

'Just testing,' Paul shouted. 'A bit loud even for a panic button.'

'A panic button?' Emma laughed. 'Who uses it? The patient when you delve too deeply into his grubby past, or you Paul?'

'Don't knock it, Sister.' Mick twisted a knob to make the sound less and tested it again. 'I got the idea from that film I saw last month when the detective was attacked and he had a device like this that saved his life.'

Emma put on a suitably impressed expression and promised to leave it alone unless she really had to summon help.

'You've never needed it, but you might,' Mick said cryptically. 'Or I might,' he grinned. 'You never know, I might get raped by that nympho who took a shine to me. Or perhaps not, if Eileen is out shopping and you are busy in the office. Let nature take its course, I say!'

'We never leave you alone with her,'

Emma said. 'And you know you wouldn't dare. She's given up fluttering her eyelashes at you and Paul and she doesn't really need to come here. She's happy as she is. It's just her rather severe father who insisted that she needed help after one or two ... incidents.'

'With that figure she's got a good career in front of her,' Mick suggested. 'Real up-market tarts earn a fortune.'

'No need to be coarse,' Paul remarked mildy. 'I can hardly tell her that her future lies in that direction.'

## Chapter Two

'It's been a long day,' Paul said. 'Let's spoil ourselves and eat out in that Italian place, but first I have a bottle of really good sherry we must try. Remember the pilot who took up medicine? He dropped by with this and told me he was married a month ago. He looks fine and is going to concentrate on medicine and not surgery, a wise choice as he need never have to tangle with the surgeon who made his life a misery. I wonder what happens to men like him who now have two careers? Would they recall him as a pilot if there is another war or would he have a dispensation to stay out of the RAF as he is a trainee doctor?'

'I think his wife might prefer him as a medical student and not a pilot.'

'Bea seemed unmoved by the thought of a war in Korea,' Paul said as he handed Emma her glass of Fino sherry.

'That's because she knows that you work miracles and would not let Dwight get past the medical board.'

'I did point out that I have no pull in American air force circles and they have their own analysts.'

'You were the one who treated Dwight here and he has plenty of influential relatives. Not every man has a godfather who is a four-star general and a family in Texas who are close to the White House in politics and contributions to the party, not to mention Bea who would be a lioness if anyone tried to take him away. At this end, Bea's father has influence too as a British Member of Parliament. It's no good saying that his case would be reviewed just on the merits of being a flyer, influence does help, however much we deplore it at times.'

'More?' He held up the bottle, then corked it firmly when she shook her head. 'Right, we'll go to Mario's and have gnocchi and whatever he has in his tagliatelle tonight.'

'Another bottle? Where did you get this one? I thought we'd used the last one that Bea's father brought over.' Emma held up the bottle of wine that Paul had put ready to take to Mario's.

'Mrs Molton this time. Marriage seems to be in the air for my ex-patients. She has a thriving business, an efficient manager, a very good-looking husband who had the sense to opt out of the factory and now works for a firm of accountants so is not ruled by the boss lady, which could have its dicey moments however much she loves him. She had a desire to say thank you, without stroking my arm!'

'You missed a really wealthy woman, darling.'

'I can still feel the mental claws, digging in each time she came here.'

Mario had mixed his images. A huge fishing net hung from the ceiling, more to hide the bad plaster that he wanted to have replaced when he could spare the

34

time and obtain the building materials, than for decoration. It served a useful purpose and caught any bits likely to fall into the food. A few Chianti bottles in raffia cases with candles in them to light the tables, added to the Italian ambiance, and a heavy millstone set on a log was now permanently covered with flour, so that it could be used to show his panache when making pizza bases before the eyes of his customers. As yet unlicensed to sell alcohol, he encouraged his regulars to bring in wine for their own tables and often sat and sampled the drink with them.

The restaurant was busy so Paul and Emma were left alone and had no need to pretend interest in the large family in Italy who all seemed to be called Mario or Maria and had in their turn innumerable children, dark and smiling in the pictures he had stuck to a leatherette screen.

Mario's English wife, a pretty blonde woman, sat by the desk, her smock barely adequate to hide her pregnant body and Emma looked away. It was bad enough having Bea asking when she would have something to tell her as she wanted sibling friends for the twins, not elderly aunts and uncles! On their last visit to the restaurant,

Mario had told them with pride about his wife's pregnancy. 'She say not yet as she is busy and has a waistline but nature said aha! and see how she swells and is bellissima, so beautiful!'

Paul filled the glasses again with the smooth red wine and watched Emma's face. Her smile was tight in spite of the relaxing wine and good food. Suddenly, she wanted to cry. He put a hand to cover hers on the table. 'You read the report.' It was a statement, not a question. 'I was furious. I told him that I wanted to collect it so that you wouldn't see it but the fool posted it and you opened it with the rest of the clinic mail.'

She nodded. A thin smile tried to appear but failed. 'At least one of us is normal.'

'I went to him so that if it was my fault that we aren't conceiving a child you would not have to have the tiresome tests done.'

'That was good of you. Most men take it for granted that it's the wife at fault and refuse to be tested in case their virility is questioned.' She swirled the last of her wine round the glass. 'I'll make an appointment at Beatties next week.'

'No need. We are happy as we are.'

'Like you, I want to know, but now it seems almost useless to have tests. They don't alter anything. They don't *do* anything; just say I am fertile or I am not.' She gave a bitter laugh. 'Poetic justice, I suppose. I was not wanted as a child and I didn't really love my parents. I thought I didn't want children, or that I wasn't maternal enough to give a baby my love, but Bea and the twins ...' She bit her lip. 'I could eat them! I want our baby, Paul. I want to look into its eyes and see you; I want to see its first smile. I want it desperately now, and everywhere I go I see pregnant girls who just blossom and I can't wait to be fat and ugly and have backache and frequency!'

'That's better. You're smiling at last. Have the test and if it's bad, we can think again, of adoption perhaps? Whatever the outcome, nothing changes. I love you and you love me and we can never let this come between us. We have a good life.'

'You're right. I'll see Stella Morgan at Beatties and I may have to stay overnight.' He raised his eyebrows. 'We'll do what's necessary,' she said firmly. Stella says it doesn't hurt to shake the tree.'

'Nice lady!'

'She does tests and then likes to push air up the fallopian tubes to see if there is a blockage there. She finds a good few of them are slightly blocked but not many gynae men think of that. An early infection from an inflamed appendix or something similar, even in a childhood fever, can make adhesions that block the tubes. If nothing more, it is one extra thing that is ruled out safely and Stella does have a record of a lot of pregnancies occurring after the tubes are shaken up a little.'

'I'll take you in.'

'No Paul, I want to saunter in as if visiting, with my toothbrush and nightie just in case.'

'After that you must go down to Aunt Emily for a few days. You work hard and need a change, apart from having this on your mind. I wish I'd never had the test done.'

'Don't say that. I had it in the back of my mind and needed this to give me a nudge in the right direction.' She sighed. 'Some people are just not lucky. Eileen has been married far longer than we have and she shows no sign of having a baby, although she adores them.'

'Unlike our treasure, Mrs Coster.'

'I know she had several children and is now on to grandchildren but I don't envy her. Maybe I should go out cleaning other people's houses. A bit of rough charring might be the answer!'

'She said when I remarked on her large family, "My old man only had to shake his trousers at the end of the bed and I was pregnant! I made him keep off the grass after our Maisie was born and if he has a bint now, it's a relief until I get the change, then I'll see her off." At least she's cheerful about it and loves them all in an offhand way.'

Emma smiled more naturally. 'Imagine any woman looking forward to the menopause so she can have sex with her husband!'

Emma cleaned the clinical room and checked linen for the consulting room the next day, as urgently as if she was going away for weeks instead of one night in hospital, and made an appointment for as soon as was possible. It was an amazing relief to discuss it with Paul and she wondered if her new, relaxed mood might do more than the examination by the leading gynaecologist at Beatties, but she kept the appointment and listened to the options open to her if she had blocked tubes.

'Forget adoption for a while,' Stella told her briskly. 'Give nature another chance and then consider insemination, if your uterus is healthy but the ova can't get there to embed safely. That way the baby would be yours and Paul's, and not some strange unrecognisable little creature whom you would love, but not quite in the same way.'

It was strange to be back in the hospital where she had served for several years during the war, and her memories flooded back with half-forgotten and sometimes poignant recollections of events during that time. They'd painted the private rooms pale blue or pale yellow now, she noticed, and each room had a telephone connection. She hoped that Paul would not ring as she'd insisted that she would get in touch when she wanted to come home, but before that she wanted to be Garbo-like, alone.

The operating theatre had a very tidy anaesthetic room smelling as usual of ether and disinfectant and the theatre sister was efficient. 'You can't fault us and say you did it better,' Stella said. She regarded her with affection. 'They aren't better, but very good and some of us remember you and Guy at the base hospital in Surrey.' She saw Emma stiffen and her eyes cloud over with emotion. 'Sorry. I'm a stupid bitch at times. I forgot he died and you married another doctor.'

Emma smiled wanly. 'I'm more interested in the future now. Paul and I have a very good marriage and coming back here to all this is like a dream, some of it good, some bad.'

The premedication injection blurred everything and Emma was glad that Stella believed in having a thoroughly relaxed patient for the insufflation of tubes in case she had to do a dilatation and curettage if the lining of the womb needed scraping.

The ceiling of her private room was banded with late winter sunlight when Emma woke, feeling stiff and slightly sore. She saw a clean white apron and felt fingers on her wrist. 'Awake? Good. Miss Morgan will be with you shortly.' The staff nurse looked sleek and attractive and Emma thought of Bea and the way she pulled her blonde hair up under her starched cap. 'Not feeling sick?' the girl asked cheerfully. 'You can have a couple

41

of pillows and one sip of water, and I think I hear Miss Morgan now.'

Not Dr Morgan as the Americans would call her. Beatties still called female surgeons 'Miss' and male surgeons 'Mr' to mark them apart from physicians, a principle that often confused many patients and now made Emma smile as she remembered surgeons who were annoyed when they were thought to be less than doctors because of this, at least by the uninitiated.

'You look cheerful.'

'I feel a bit sore but not enough to worry me, Stella.'

'I didn't have to scrape you. Perfectly healthy in there but the gauge showed some resistance to the air in both tubes and then the dial suddenly adjusted to normal in one so we may have found a blockage and dealt with it, at least on one side and possibly the interference opened the other one. Stay here tonight as you probably feel tired and Paul will fetch you at nine tomorrow morning.' She laughed. 'He's a charmer. Guy was a dish but over the phone I sensed a warmth that Guy never had. Paul will give you nicer babies.'

'I think so too if we are lucky.'

'Give yourself a year Emma. Just forget you ever had a problem and let time sort you out, but if it doesn't, come back to me.' Stella pulled the curtains across the window. 'Go back to sleep and I'll say goodbye now. Paul can look after you at home. Take a Codeine if you have an ache in there, a day or so taking things easy, and back to a normal love life.'

'That sounds simple. Thank you and goodbye.' Emma snuggled down, comforted and blissfully sleepy. I'll go down to the Island, she promised herself.

'I'm not likely to break in half,' Emma protested feebly when Paul held the car door open and tucked her into the passenger seat with care, but her eyes were bright as she saw his deep commitment.

'I rang Aunt Emily and she'll have the cottage aired out by Thursday, so all you have to do is pack and take a train.'

'There's a lot to do here. Perhaps I'd better wait for a few weeks.'

'No arguments! It will soon be Christmas and I want us to be here for that this year. There are a lot of people we haven't seen since Bea's going away party and the hospital has invited us to a few functions.' He parked the car by the front door of the house and handed the small overnight bag to Emma before driving off to put the car in the garage at the back of the house.

He saw her reflection in the rear-view mirror, her back straight and slim and graceful and he sighed. Many men would like to change places with him, children or no children and he wanted his wife to be away from the Island before her cousin George came home on leave from the Navy. Aunt Emily had told him that George and his mother Janey would be bringing Clive, his small son, to her for Christmas at the house near Shide on the Isle of Wight.

'Janey wasn't all that keen, I could tell, as her husband likes his own bed and his workshop to potter in even when he's not supposed to be working, and she invited me to go there to stay, but George begged me to invite them months ago, and as you know, Alex can refuse nothing that George wants now that Sadie is dead and he and Janey have George's nice little boy to look after. It's made Janey ten years younger.' Emily had paused as if unsure what to say.

'I'd like Emma to come to you for a few days but to be back here by next week,' Paul said firmly. 'I'm glad you didn't ask us to come for Christmas. Emma misses Bea and the twins and I think that seeing little Clive just now might be a mistake, as it would remind her how fond she is of the twins.'

'That's what I thought.' She sounded relieved, as if Paul would think this reason enough.

'And?'

Emily laughed. 'No point in stirring the pot is there? George thought you'd both be here with me but it wouldn't be good for him either. He still loves Emma. You know that. It's time he found another wife and it's time that you had children of your own!'

'We're working on it,' Paul said mildly. 'We've had tests and Emma had a little treatment and needs a break, so wish us luck.'

'Send her down and I'll say nothing unless she likes to talk about it,' she promised. 'I'll get Wilf's lad to put her car at the end of the pier so she can drive to your cottage, or maybe it would be better if she stays with me as I shall be alone then. Pity to waste the fuel,' she added briskly; and a pity to leave her feeling lonely at the cottage, was what she thought.

'Bless you, Aunt Emily.' He laughed. 'You usually manage to work some magic. How about fertility spells?'

'I am not a witch! I just have a bit more common sense than most people.'

'You knew when Sadie was going to die.' His voice was quiet but had a trace of real anxiety.

'There's nothing bad for you or Emma. She's so close that I'd know if there was anything to worry about concerning her, but I have a feeling that there might be a worry about someone to do with your home. Not family,' she added.

'Mick is afraid he might be called up again if there is war in Korea.'

'Maybe that's it.' But Paul wondered if that was really what she saw in her fey mind.

Emma made coffee. 'I didn't bother with breakfast as you were collecting me early and I wasn't really hungry.'

'That makes two of us. If I put some

bread in the toaster and we stand ready with knives and butter and marmalade to eat it hot, do you think it might taste better than the last lot of grey cardboard we ate?'

'I'll ask Eileen to make soda bread for lunch,' she promised.

'Everything OK?'

'In a peculiar way I enjoyed it. I caught up with a lot of gossip with Stella, and I could start there again tomorrow if she had her way. They need a new sister in gynae theatre but I said no, I want to stay here.'

'Good. I have other plans for you, but it's as well that you are going away now. I love you so much, but I know I must wait.' He kissed her and she was suddenly desperate that someday, they'd have their dream come true and she would carry his child.

'You can't get rid of me quickly enough,' she teased him. 'Aunt Emily and you have me all tied up between you. I think you ought to come with me as it's really you she wants to see.'

'Some of us are too busy to go away to a delightful place and eat Emily's lovely grub. When you come back, just say nothing about rabbit stew with herby dumplings or bramley apple pie with illegal cream.'

'I'll try to buy some Lower's pork pies,' she promised. 'They are the only bought pies that Emily will eat as she says she knows who makes them and where the pork comes from. I'll take a waterproof bag too, in case Dr Sutton has a few gifts of rabbits or a boiling fowl from grateful patients, that he can spare.'

Eileen came to fetch a clean jug for the milk that would be delivered soon. She divided it each day, some for her own flat and the rest for Emma's use. 'You still have a pint and a half, so I'll make you a rice pudding for tonight. Dr Paul doesn't eat enough when you are away.'

'Make sure he does for the next few days, Eileen. I'm going down to visit my aunt and so he'll probably starve if you don't feed him.'

'I'd never let that happen.'

'You see, you will not notice I'm away.'

'I shall if we have Miss Stanley here again,' Eileen said with feeling. 'I don't mind sitting in the consulting room with

Dr Paul, acting as chaperone when he has women patients, but she is strange!'

Paul laughed. 'I'll ask Mick to stay with us the next time, he said. 'She doesn't fancy men.'

'You mean she fancies women?' The idea seemed to fascinate Eileen. 'I've never come across that before. That's why she likes me to help her on with her cardigan and the last time she was here, she kissed my cheek and tried to hug me.'

'Quite harmless and she can't help her feelings. She does need help with her obsessional hand washing and a few other hang-ups, but Mick might be a better chaperone from now on when she has an appointment, and I'll introduce him as your husband!'

Eileen frowned. 'I think Mick might need you soon. He's a bit cracked himself.'

'Mick?' Emma giggled. 'Quite the most down to earth creature I've met. He is so level-headed he makes me feel positively bird-brained.'

'He practises walking funny. He even uses a stick as if he needs it but he can run like a rabbit when he wants to.'

Emma and Paul exchanged glances.

They had both heard of men who wanted to hide behind an imagined injury or pain to gain sympathy, but Mick was well adjusted and had the love of a good wife and the affection of his employers and no financial worries.

Eileen blushed as if she wanted to talk but hated being disloyal. 'He took your lovely curly stick when he went to see his CO. When I went on to him about it he said it was better than his old one and would make a better impression.'

'Has he talked about going back to the army?'

'Funny you should say that. He had a letter from his old oppo. You know, the one who came here after his leg was taken out of plaster. His case was reassessed for duty on the reserve. Not that it means he will go back into the army but it made Mick mad. He said they had their discharges and the army had no right to call them up again.'

'Have they asked him to appear before a board?'

'No, but I think that his old CO wanted to have a few hand-picked sergeants ready if he needed them. That's what Mick thought when he went to that weekend in Surrey.'

'What did he say when he came back?' Paul was amused. 'I thought he looked rather pleased.'

'He said that his old CO told him he could do with men like him at this side if war came again, but however much Mick wanted to go, he must realise that it was impossible. Some of the men were all stirred up and wanted to be called up on the reserve now, but Mick doesn't seem to be disappointed at all at what the officer said.'

'Had Mick said he wanted to go?' Emma tried to hide her disbelief.

'That's the funny thing. His CO obviously thought he did want to be on the reserve, but when I asked Mick, he said, "Over my dead body," and grinned as if he had got his own way.'

'Crafty old devil,' Paul said. 'Take him my curly stick and say he can keep it until his legs are better, and don't worry about him. He has never been saner. Maybe not entirely honest, but quite sane. Our gain and the army's loss. He won't be going to Korea now or later and you can forget it, Eileen.'

# Chapter Three

'Put the kettle on', said Emily Darwen's scribbled message. Emma poked the fire and put on a small cherry log, then went into the neat kitchen and filled the kettle. It was three o'clock in the afternoon and she knew that Emily would be back from Dr Sutton's surgery at any time now. As usual in that house, an air of calm pervaded the atmosphere and she sank into an armchair in front of the fire and began to read the *Isle of Wight County Press,* the local newspaper printed every week.

She read the account of a farm accident, a visit from an industrialist from the mainland who wanted to build a controversial estate of houses and was having resistance from the local council who wanted the land for a municipal building, and a case in the local magistrate's court of a man who had stolen a bucket of vegetables and a garden fork from an allotment and had been sentenced to a small fine but also admonished to go back to Portsmouth where he came from, as 'we don't want your sort over here!'

It was cosy and very parochial and comforting to know that crime had not made many dents in the local scene.

'When you come to the obituaries, see if I'm there.'

'Aunt Emily!' Emma put aside the paper and hugged her aunt. 'Not you. You are immortal. Kettle's boiling. Are you ready for tea?'

'We all die,' Emily said succinctly. 'Did you ever know a time when I didn't want a cup? Let me look at you.' She nodded approval. 'Make the tea; I've made a sponge with strawberry jam filling to go with it.'

'Bea would enjoy this,' Emma said.

'She makes one as good as I can. She insisted that she couldn't live without Victoria sponge cake in America and she made me teach her that and how to make proper fluffy dumplings that aren't like lead bullets, as Dwight likes them.'

'She sends her love and so does Dwight. He thinks they could do with you in Washington where you'd show some important people a bit of Isle of Wight common sense. The twins are fine

53

and take up a lot of Bea's time as she wants them brought up well and to know that she is their mother, unlike her own experience when she was left to a series of nannies and servants and hardly knew her parents. They still have their English nanny so there is always someone reliable to take over if Bea has to accompany Dwight to receptions and other formal occasions.'

'They'll do, and so will the twins.'

'I'll tell her what you said and she'll feel safe.'

'Why should she feel otherwise? The war has been over for quite a time and they say that things are getting better, even if they don't look like it sometimes.' She regarded Emma with shrewd but tender eyes. 'Everything comes to those who wait patiently.'

'Everything?'

'If you're a good girl and eat up your greens, as my mother used to say. We do need some sprouts picked, so if you'd do that, I'll get the pork in the oven and peel the potatoes.'

'Dr Sutton had a grateful patient?'

'Almost a whole side of pork, apart from the leg. He suspects that the farmer wanted to get it out of his farmhouse in case the inspector saw it and accused him of killing more than his quota, or whatever the regulations are now. He sent over a hand of pork for us when he heard you were coming and was disappointed that Paul wouldn't be with you.'

'Does he think there will be another war?'

'Not close to home. Janey worries in case George is sent to the Far East where trouble seems to be ever present, but that's up to the Americans this time for a change, and the unarmed United Nations troops keep an eye on peacekeeping, or so George says.'

'He's coming here for Christmas?'

Emily put chopped onions and rings of apple in the baking dish and scored the pork skin before rubbing it well with salt. She poured dry cider round the meat and added a few leaves of fresh sage and parsley, then put the dish in the oven.

'George *is* coming to you?' Emma remarked when Emily chose to ignore her. 'We haven't seen him for a very long time. He came to London a while back but I was at Beatties visiting a friend and I missed seeing him then, so I would like to see him now.'

'If I have anything to do with it you'll not see him for another long time.'

'Aunt Emily! He is back to normal. I know he must miss Sadie, but he has Clive and Janey and you and a very busy life in the Navy. I can't imagine him brooding over me. There was never anything between us and we agreed that it would be nice to keep in touch as cousins, which is what we are.'

'Who agreed?' Emily sniffed. 'He had no option.'

'Isn't he happy?'

'Up to a point, but he's careful who he lets into his life now. Sadie was a frothy girl who never wanted children. George took her for her looks when he really wanted you, and if he marries again he needs a more mature woman who will love Clive and perhaps give him more children, but he doesn't need you looking smart and pretty and being bright and ... comforting, even if it is your stock-in-trade for difficult patients,' she added dryly. 'How many of Paul's disturbed men fall for you, I wonder?'

'Not many.' Emma laughed. 'It's the women I have to watch with Paul. He needs a chaperone quite often and I have to sit in with him.'

'Pick the sprouts before it gets dark and you can tell me all about that. I like a bit of scandal.'

'And when you have Aunt Janey here, you'll sit by the fire with your awful, strong whisky-laced tea and tell her about it!'

'Only the bits that don't hurt anybody,' Emily replied. 'No secrets.'

'Paul told you about me?'

'I said I wouldn't mention it until you did, but I knew you would tell me sooner or later. Can't say your looks pity you. How do you feel?'

'Fine, apart from being disappointed. I'll pick the sprouts.'

The smell of cooking drifted across the garden, and in the dusk Emma trod on a bed of sage that sent its bitter odour into the moist air. She resolved to take a plant back with her to replace the one that had died in the rubble-filled soil of Kensington. Here, Wilf could bring loads of good manure from the farms to feed the garden but she couldn't think where to get any in London, unless Mrs Coster knew a man with a horse and cart who worked in the markets.

Two huge upturned clay flower pots resting on pieces of wood made her curious and she looked under one of them at fresh green leaves that she didn't recognise. Carefully she replaced the pot as the plants were obviously something that Aunt Emily valued. It was too dark now to examine them closely, but in the morning, she went into the garden again to pick a cabbage and fetch a few potatoes from the clump behind the shed and she saw small buds that hung down on slender stems.

'What are under the earthenware pots?' she asked as Emily sat with her, eating toast and drinking far more strong tea than was good for her.

'Christmas roses. They have a fancy name but we always called them that. Mother liked to have a plant or two as the flowers last well in a cold room in winter, and have a nice, mild scent. They bloom too late for autumn and too early for spring, so they are very welcome when we can get no other flowers except chrysanthemums"

'I'd like to take some home. Are they difficult to grow?'

Emily smiled in a way that was secret and amusing to her. 'They take time to be established and then seem to go on blooming every winter for ever.'

'If they are to bloom at Christmas they don't seem very well advanced.'

'Not this year. This is the first year I've had them and they need to put down roots and mature. The flowers will be small at first and not worth picking but next year, who knows what will bloom?'

'So you have to wait until next Christmas when you will have some to pick?'

'Christmas roses never bloom in time for Christmas. They come a little later, in January or February and we keep them protected from the rain which muddies them, as they are close to the ground.'

'So you can't even enjoy them in the garden? Let's hope they are worth all your care and attention.'

'Most things that cause a bit of trouble or heartache are worth waiting for.'

'I hope you are right.' Emma spoke softly, with a trace of a sadness. 'I don't mind waiting, if it isn't too long.'

'You said you'd take me into Newport,' Emily said briskly. 'Cook that cabbage now, and with last night's leftover potatoes we can make colcannon for supper with the cold pork and pickles. Make plenty as Dr

Sutton is fond of it and I take him a bit now and then.'

'And apple pie and cake and a few pasties.'

'He's a good man and his housekeeper has a very heavy hand with pastry.'

Clouds threatened rain but the trip to Newport passed well, and they returned with oranges and bananas, fruit that had made a reappearance after the war, which many children had never seen or tasted until the banana boats could bring them safely to England again, without having to be escorted by naval convoys.

'It still seems wrong to have to buy fish after the years my father sold it in the shop on Coppins Bridge. We had plenty to eat when we lived there, even in the First World War, and after she got married, my sister Lizzy was so angry when Mother sold up. She never came to help Mother, but visited and took away as much of the vegetables and fish as she could carry from the shop and never paid a penny for it. I think she sold it on to her neighbours but Mother turned a blind eye and said she needed it as she married a mean man.'

'Did that aunt have children?'

'One, a boy. You met your cousin once

when you were small and you didn't like him,' Emily said. 'He whined and had a runny nose.'

'What happened to him?'

'He works on the mainland and his parents died two years ago. I didn't tell you as it was no use pretending to miss them, but I went to the funerals. Lizzie's husband died first and when I asked if she missed him a lot, she said with that sniff I hated so much, "He was useful for bringing in the coal", so I stopped worrying about that one!'

'So you never see my cousin?'

'He doesn't want me and I have never liked him. I was more fond of the ones who were far away, like your uncle Sidney in America and Edward, who became a stationmaster and eventually took his wife to Rhodesian Railways where he did very well. They stayed out there after he retired. She had a sweet nature but was ill for most of her youth with diabetes and Mother did a lot for her, but when they discovered insulin they saved her life. Rose was like the cracked pot at the well; she outlasted a lot of more healthy people. She was often difficult but I was fond of her. She had that lovely pink and white skin so her name suited her—Rose.'

'You are close to Aunt Janey but not to my mother.' Emma packed away the groceries and put the fruit in a crystal bowl on the sideboard.

'Clare was Lizzie's twin and out of the same mould. I think that even my mother who loved us all, thought that nature had played a trick on her giving her that pair. Clare was a selfish girl and had no time for anyone but herself, even after she married.' Emily stirred the colcannon and added a lump of butter from the pat that a friend had brought from his farm at Chale.

'That's a lot of butter.'

'Take some back with you. He brings more than I can eat.' She stirred again, avoiding looking directly at Emma. 'I wanted to talk about Clare. What happens when she is ill and when she dies?'

'Paul says we must take her in if she needs help,' Emma said shortly. 'He has never met her as she refused to come to our wedding and has ignored any letters I sent after that. She never forgave me for refusing to marry Phillip. She thought it was stupid to say I wouldn't marry him, as I would have had a good allowance as an RAF officer's widow if he died in the service. Actually she resented me marrying anyone as she wanted me at her beck and call for life, but Phillip buttered her up hoping that it would influence me!'

'I've thought about Clare lately, more than any time over the war years. I asked her down here once but she said she was busy with her real friends so I gave up.'

'She didn't need any financial help as my father provided for her very well and there is no mortgage on the house. She has this awful woman from the chapel who has made her believe that she is the only one who likes her and who can be trusted, which may be true,' Emma added. 'She used to stir up trouble between Mother and my father, as if there wasn't trouble enough there already, and she hates men. If she had the courage she'd have been a lesbian but Mother never liked physical contact of any kind so that wasn't likely.'

'You do have the address of her solicitor and doctor? Do they have yours? Clare was always slap-happy over legal matters.'

Emma felt cold. 'What are you saying? Have you heard that she is ill?'

Emily's dark brown eyes were sad. 'No, I've heard nothing, but someday we all die Emma, and I dream of her a lot now.

She is a good few years older than me. I was the youngest in our family of seven children.'

'Do you think I should do something? Go to see her? Write again? The last letter I had from her said I'd only got in touch because I was hard up and wanted something and she didn't wish to be involved. Her words were, "I don't care whatever is wrong that caused you to write to me. You've made your bed and must lie on it. You've not been a daughter to me ever since you went to London and left me." She was quoting Mrs Hammond. I could almost hear that old harridan's voice.'

'No need for you to do anything, but I think I'll drop a line to her doctor, saying we have lost touch, and if there is any crisis and she needs help, he can telephone me here.' Emily looked pensive. 'I'll write to her solicitor, too.'

'Why bother? She has probably made a will leaving everything to the chapel or that woman.' Emma tried to laugh. 'This is awful, discussing my own mother as if she is dead!'

'Forget we talked about it. I'll see to it. Now then, there's a nice film at the

Medina. We could go there tonight after supper.'

'Let's do that.' Emma wanted to shake off the sudden depression she felt, not because her mother had nothing in common with her only daughter but because Emily might be hurt more than she admitted if anything bad happened to another of her family.

Emma didn't say that she had seen the film in London, as Emily was entranced by the singing and the thin story of *State Fair*, but thought that farm people wouldn't dress like that if they had to drive carts and pick crops. It was all light-hearted and innocent and they returned to the warm house ready for bed, very well content.

At breakast, Emma brought in the mail and set the envelopes next to Emily's cup, then cut the homemade loaf. Emily put on her half glasses and eyed her niece over the top. 'That is from Janey. George is coming home a few days early and they'll all be here tomorrow.'

'Shall I make some cake and more bread?'

'No, you pack your bag my girl.'

'I can help. There must be lots to do before they come, and I can go down to the cottage tonight to free my room here. It will be nice to see Aunt Janey again and Clive must have grown a lot. Are they bringing a car? I suppose they will have to with all Clive's things but if not I can meet their ferry.'

'You won't be here,' Emily said firmly. 'I'm not having George mooning over you even for one day, so you'll have to get back to London.'

'I was enjoying this so much.'

'There'll be many other times, very happy times, and I want to see Paul next time.'

Her gentle tone made Emma smile. 'I'll go! Just because you prefer men, and Paul in particular, doesn't make me jealous, but I think you are seeing far more than is true about George.' She finished her breakfast and went into the garden where Wilf was chopping wood. 'I have to go back, so would you drive me to the ferry this morning?'

'Did she throw you out? You only got here five minutes ago!' He put his axe on the heap of wood and went to wash his hands and find out if Emily needed any shopping in Ryde on his way back.

He found her in the kitchen reading

the letter from Janey again. 'George is taking a few extra days' leave and says he can't wait to get here to see us all. On the phone, he asked when Emma and Paul would arrive and is anxious to show Clive to them now that he is walking. Pity, but she has to go back.' Wilf nodded and picked up her shopping list. Emily shrugged. Time enough to tell them that Emma would not be spending Christmas with them on the Island, when she was safely back in her own home. Christmas was a sentimental time and even Emma might be more vulnerable just now.

Wilf left her at the pier head and turned the car towards Ryde. Emma stared back at the town and felt sad. George was a wonderful person and she would like to be friends as she felt a true sense of kinship with him, but she saw the sense of keeping away just now. One Christmas had been eventful, before Bea and Dwight went to America, when George and Sadie had been there too. The fact that George had been in love with her before he married the pretty American girl might bring back bitter dregs of memory and memories were dangerous things. Far better for George to spend his time with his son and his mother and find the peace that Emily thought had evaded him.

Mick was at the station and waved as soon as he saw her. 'Dr Paul said you'd be on this one. What's up? Had enough of seagulls and salt water?' He glanced at her and grinned. 'Or was the pace too hot for you with sailors coming home on leave?'

'Only one sailor, his small son and his mother and stepfather, so they needed my room,' she replied with dignity.

'Yeah! I've got eyes.'

'You see too much and half of it isn't there! I wonder that Paul puts up with you.'

'He'll be glad to see you back again. He gets restless with you away. Don't we all?'

'Is something wrong?'

Mick drove past a top-heavy truck and looked puzzled. 'Don't think so, but Eileen is under the weather. We ate the same things yesterday and she is never sick as a rule but this morning she felt really ill and I left her in bed.'

'I'll take a look at her and make something bland for her supper,' Emma promised. First, she went up to see Paul who was waiting for a patient who was usually so late that Paul booked him in the diary for at least half an hour later than he usually told his patient to arrive.

'You are a sight for sore eyes,' he said when he'd kissed her.

'I was only away a day!' she laughed. 'What tragedy happened during that time, apart from Eileen having an upset stomach?'

'Mick told you?'

'He seemed a bit anxious so I said I'd have a look at her and make her something light for supper. If she has a temperature she must stay in bed for a day or so.'

'Don't go yet.'

'You look worried.' She sat in the chair by the consulting couch and looked up at him.

'Not worried, but anxious that you will not be upset. It's too early after the hospital visit for us to know if we are likely to have a child, and if Eileen is, as I think, pregnant, you must steel yourself to say all the right things and even in your heart you must not resent the fact that she will have a baby and maybe you can't.'

'I wouldn't be like that,' she began, but felt scalding tears of frustration begin to flow and she buried her face in Paul's jacket.

'See what I mean?' he said gently. 'I felt the same when I came to the conclusion that she had morning sickness, but Eileen is our friend as well as our housekeeper, a part of our family Emma, and she needs us now.'

She dashed away her tears and smiled shakily. 'All over now, but I think I'll have a cup of tea before I see her. You are wonderful Paul. I might have been shocked and shown it if you hadn't told me.'

Paul poured tea from the old Bakelite insulated teapot that kept tea hot for longer than any other and had its origins in wartime when tea was needed at all times to keep up morale. 'I made some after Mick left for the station as I knew when you'd be here. Tell me, has Aunt Emily broken the bad habit of a lifetime and given it up?'

Emma sipped her tea and smiled. 'She drinks it morning, noon and night and sent her love to you, but she turned me out when she heard that George was on the way to the Island and made no bones about it! I am forbidden to see him for a very long time. I think it's silly but she was very fierce and definite, so I came away.'

'Wise old owl. It wasn't silly at all.

George needs to be with his son and his close friends and to make a few new ones, but you would not be a good neutral companion just yet. From where I am standing you are a very desirable woman, the woman I love and who fills my life. Children would be good, but you give me enough joy to last a lifetime and I never cry for the moon or the unknown.'

'Thank you, darling,' she sighed. 'I'm fine and I'll see Eileen now. If she is expecting a baby then it's wonderful. She had almost given up hope, as they've been married for so long.'

He kissed her again. 'That's my brave, generous girl.'

'Remembering Bea at that stage, Eileen will now feel ravenous until tomorrow morning! I'll take her some of my precious cake.' She said ruefully, 'All this and heavenly cake too.'

'I thought you were keeping that fruit cake for a special occasion, like Christmas Day.'

'This is it. For Eileen, Christmas has come sooner than she expected. It is really wonderful news and now that I can face it I shall do all I can for her.'

Soon, she thought, there will be a baby

crying again in this house. I can lend her the small wicker cot that Bea thought she'd use until she found she was carrying twins. Mick can make a stand for it and Eileen can trim it.

She gulped, then smiled, picked up the cake tin and went down to see the proud couple.

## Chapter Four

Mick regarded his wife with a mixture of disbelief and triumph. 'Crikey,' he said for the third time, then to hide most of his feelings, 'haven't been having a roll with the milkman, have you? I never thought I had it in me after all this time.'

'No I haven't! And not so much of what you have done. I'm the one with sickness and all the pain of having a baby,' Eileen said, but smiled delightedly and stuffed more cake into her mouth.

'Steady on! I have to put up with you puking every morning and looking like a dying duck in a thunderstorm and then eating us out of house and home! Still,

I don't think I'll trade you in for a better model.' He reached for the plate but she got there first and finished the last crumbs. 'Don't expectant fathers have any cake?'

'That happens to be our Christmas cake,' Emma said severely. 'I shall dole it out in slices so that Eileen doesn't go mad and eat the lot.'

'Well, I have work to do,' Mick said. 'Leave the polishing, Eileen. I can do that later and you can do the interesting jobs like washing the vegetables and sewing the buttons on my shirt.'

'Mick is right,' Emma said when Eileen objected. 'Nothing heavy until you are over the first three months and then you can do anything, within reason, as the exercise will be good for you.'

She could hear her own voice as if it came from a stranger but it was her professional, nursing voice and one behind which she could hide her envy and a kind of sorrow that must not show itself to the happy couple now beaming at her as if she had something to do with the miracle of Eileen being pregnant.

'It's being here and feeling safe, Sister. My mother always used to say that nature

73

knew best when a baby could be born safely.'

Emma shook her head in denial but Mick eyed her seriously. 'She's right. A proper little nest we've built down there and all the good food and sense of security must have something to do with it.'

'That's it. I feel so safe, as if nothing can happen to hurt me or my baby now, and Mick heard from his old CO this morning.'

Emma looked surprised. 'Were you expecting to hear from him so soon? You were with him only a few days ago.'

Mick laughed. 'A very nice letter, really. When I went to his place in Surrey, I knew he wanted to look all his old lot over to see who would go with him if we had to fight again. It was cunning, as we all had a lot to say to each other about the old days and it was good to get together. A lot of people said they missed the life in the Forces. His grub wasn't bad either. It was a real softening up process. When we got there he talked a lot about the United Nations and what they did to try to keep the peace in dicey situations and some of the lads were all for it. The way he put it, it sounded a doddle. Just wear a pale blue beret and stand around and smile! No guns, no protection needed as we would be neutral, men hand-picked from all the peace-loving nations and having a great time with our pals while the two factions in Korea beat the hell out of each other.'

'We aren't at war, even if General MacArthur seems a bit restless in Japan,' Emma asserted.

'The ones in the know see it coming and my CO was always there in the front of everything. He's a natural professional fighter and I think he'd rather be in at the deep end again, not just in a refereeing position. Just now he thinks that MacArthur has got it right, even if he is an American, and can't see that he might be a warmonger who will sacrifice a lot of men to get the glory he wants.'

'What did he say in the letter?'

'Nice of him. He seemed embarrassed as he knew I must want to join him when the crunch came. Shoulder to shoulder with my friends and all that malarkey. He regretted that it was obvious that I could not go back to active service although he respected the brave face I put on my injuries. He'd seen my attempts to walk easily but no soldier could take a walking stick to help him on manoeuvres, so for all time I am now a civilian and I have his letter to prove it.'

'Surely that curly walking stick would strike terror into any enemy,' Emma suggested teasingly. 'It could look good if you stood there in a blue beret and smiled at the fighting forces.'

Mick looked stern. 'They don't know what they'd be letting themselves in for. What happens in your average fight? Someone tries to separate them and who gets clobbered? The poor stupid bastard who intervenes, that's who.'

'Keep the stick in case you get a visit from someone less trusting, who comes to check on you or asks you to attend a formal reassessment board.'

Mick laughed. 'The boss has already sent in a formal report, assessing me on his own observations, so it's all tied up now, but I will keep the stick for a while, just in case someone does remember what a devious sod I can be at times.'

'Language!' Eileen looked disapproving. 'You'll have to watch your mouth when the baby comes. We don't want her to hear such words from her own father.'

'Him!' Mick said. 'It will be a boy.'

'Maybe there are *some* things that you can't fiddle to suit yourself,' Emma said with a touch of irony.

'We do owe you and the doctor a lot,' he said, and she had a feeling that the sharp eyes hadn't missed her own hidden sadness. 'Will you tell Mrs Miller the news when you write?'

'She'll be thrilled.' Slowly Emma went up to the consulting room and Paul raised an eyebrow in query. She nodded and gave a reassuring smile and sat in her chair, slightly out of sight of the woman patient, ready to fetch and carry or make her more comfortable on the couch.

Emma noticed that she was lying on a clean sheet that didn't belong to the clinic and her head rested on a cushion that she had never seen before today. The notes indicated that the woman had an obsession with cleanliness and she had brought her own covering for the couch because she thought that others had used it, even though she knew that the linen was changed between patients.

Miss Stanley moved restlessly and her fingers picked at her clean white blouse. 'I need to go to the toilet,' she said, apologetically.

'You've been there twice since you came here today. The last time you went was ten minutes ago,' Paul pointed out. 'If you suffer from frequency, then you need to have the cause investigated, so Sister will take a sample that we can send to the pathological laboratory to see what causes it.'

'There's nothing wrong with my bladder,' she said indignantly. 'I just want to wash my hands.'

'I asked you to make a note each time you did that,' Paul told her. 'I see that you haven't brought me a note, so how many times was it yesterday?'

'I don't remember.'

'You do remember. Was it ten times?' She shook her head.

'More than twenty?'

'About that.'

'And in the night?'

'Only five times last night as I took one of the sleeping pills you gave me.' She sounded accusing, as if Paul had deprived her of something she needed to do.

'The last time you came here we talked but couldn't find the cause of this, but we discussed the possibility of me helping you sleep and asking you questions while you

78

are half asleep. Have you decided? It's entirely up to you if you want me to find what's making you have this obsession with cleanliness. You admit that it is an embarrassment when you are with friends; you can't go far alone and you have restless nights.'

'I am very tired,' she admitted. 'Sometimes my hands are so sore with the washing that I can hardly bear them in water, but if I put cream on them, I feel that I must scrub it off again. My GP says I'll end up with a bad dermatitis if I go on like this.' She clasped tensed hands in front of her. 'I don't like the idea of losing control of my own mind but go ahead. I can't go on much longer like this. I'm at the stage when I'll try anything.'

Emma lowered the head of the couch so that Miss Stanley was reclining comfortably and saw that she gave a sigh of resignation as if she thought that whatever Dr Sykes did would be comforting, but would have no lasting effect for good. Paul used thiopentone to produce a hypnotic state and Emma held the hand of the now relaxed woman.

He asked mundane questions about her present style of living and about her house, then asked her to think back to last year. 'Did you suffer in this way before last Christmas?'

'Yes, and for a long time before that, but it was not as bad and very few people noticed what I did.'

'Why did you come to me?'

'My GP suggested you and my house-keeper threatened to leave if I didn't get help. I can't do without her so I came.'

'Go back a little more. Did anything happen to you during the war?' She tensed and said nothing, and Paul repeated the question with a tone of authority.

'We were bombed.' The words came slowly, reluctantly.

'We were all bombed, so what was special about *you* being bombed? Let's go to that day or night when it happened to you.' He pushed the plunger of the syringe slightly and she relaxed more deeply. 'The air-raid siren has gone. Where are you?'

'In the office.'

'So you are in an office when the bombs begin to fall. What are you doing? Did you hear the siren and go to the shelter or stay in the office? Describe it for me.'

'I was in the office where I worked for an army charity and we went down to the ground floor where they said it was safer.' She began to breathe rapidly. 'Two air-raid wardens sat playing cards under a slung staircase as there was no cellar or air-raid shelter close to the office building. They had been through many raids and felt safe. We had brown paper strips crisscrossing on the windows I remember, to catch broken glass in case of blast from an explosion, and the doorway was protected by sand bags piled high. The wardens had made sure that everyone was out of the top floor and we waited for the all clear; someone even went to the kitchen to make tea.'

She shuddered. 'What happened? Do you remember the noise? Did you have any warning?' Paul asked.

'It came across the sky making a roaring noise and one of the men said it was a buzz-bomb on its way past the city and his friend laughed and said it didn't have his name on it and shuffled the cards again. Then the noise stopped and we knew it was about to fall. It had sounded a long a way off but the silence now was almost as frightening as the roaring noise.'

Emma hoped that her own hand was not as tense as she felt. She recalled the buzz-bombs and the most dangerous time after the engine stopped and it took a wide parabola, landing a long way off from the end of the noise. If it cut out overhead, the people under it were safe, but others further on would have the full force of the explosion.

Paul's voice was flat and unmoved. 'The bomb fell on the office?'

'Yes,' she whispered.

'Where were you?'

'I was sitting on a stool by a filing cabinet and a stack of books and stationery, looking across at the wardens. I thought they had seated themselves in the safest place under the stairs, where they went each time the siren sounded, leaving us to find our own safe places. Typical of men, I thought, then the bomb exploded.'

'Describe what you saw.'

Emma looked up anxiously, wondering if Paul was going too far, as Miss Stanley was pale and wriggled uncomfortably as if to get away from something terrible.

'Dust and falling bricks,' she said, almost as if it was a dream. 'Everywhere, dust, and then screaming, and another blast when the gas in the kitchen exploded. The girl making the tea was badly scalded by boiling water. The stairs had collapsed and the metal struts that had kept them up had fallen on the wardens. The pile of books and paper protected me but the force of the blast threw one man into the air, and his body fell on top of me.' She began to weep softly.

'It's over now and you are not hurt by the bomb.' Paul's voice was sharp. 'Tell me what happened next.'

'Blood ... and a smell of faeces ... so much blood all over my hands and face and flesh coming away from his body.' She dragged her hands away from Emma and started to move them one over the other as if washing them.

Paul put her into a deeper trance-like state and she relaxed again. 'They've washed away the blood now and you are clean. They've washed it all away and you have changed your clothes and helped to tidy the office.' She nodded and smiled. He went on, 'They've taken away the dead man and the others who were wounded, the smell has gone and you are safe.'

'I am alive.' She sounded surprised.

'You are alive and clean, the blood has gone completely and for ever, so there is no need to wash more than twice a day. Do you hear me? Repeat what I have said.'

'I have no need to wash more than twice a day.' The words were dragged out and her face was contorted as if under duress.

'I will waken you now and you will forget what has happened here in this room, but you will gradually lose your anxiety about washing.'

Emma slipped away to make tea and when she returned, Paul was sitting in her chair and smiling. Miss Stanley sat on the couch, looking bemused and Emma helped her to put on her shoes.

'Did I fall asleep?'

'For a while.'

'I feel tired, but I've lost the headache I had earlier today when I knew I was coming here.'

'Milk and sugar?' Emma asked, as if Paul had concluded a normal and entertaining conversation with his patient.

'You are both very kind, but I can't think you did any good, Doctor, if I was asleep all the time.'

'We made progress but you need to have another appointment. I have found something in your past life during the war that has a lot to do with your condition but we must go slowly because you had forgotten it. Don't force yourself to remember things that you went through during the war. Just take life easy and come back next week for a little more hypnosis.'

'Let me put your sheet and pillow in your bag,' Emma said. 'More tea?' Miss Stanley accepted another cup and Paul looked interested. On her previous visit she had refused tea and said she never drank anything away from home, drinking from cups that other people had used.

'Sit there until you feel fit to leave,' Emma smiled reassuringly.

'My friend is fetching me. She may be here now.'

'Good.' Paul shook her hand. 'If you want to tidy up before you leave, you know where the cloakroom is.'

'I'm all right. My hair isn't untidy, is it Sister?'

'You look fine. I was admiring your suit. It looks like a Hardy Amies model and I love the colour.'

'How clever of you to know!'

They went down to the front entrance chatting about clothes and when she had gone, Emma found Paul in the office.

'She didn't use the wash basin!'

'I know, but we haven't cured her yet. She will need to remember what happened and that will be a trauma that I hate to impose on her, but it will clear her psyche and bring her back to normal.'

'Poor soul. Some women have a lot to bear. My needs seem irrelevant now.'

'I disagree, but we are going to beat it.' Paul laughed. 'With Eileen pregnant, who knows? It may be catching.'

'So they say,' Emma replied and wondered, if that was so, why hadn't it happened when Bea had her twins?'

'Do you need Mick for anything?' Paul asked later. 'I told him to take the car and see Eileen off to the antenatal clinic. I want to make sure she is being looked after by her own GP and a good hospital and only asks my advice in an emergency. I don't want to try to mix obstetrics with psychiatry! I might end up on an analyst's couch myself.'

'I was glad that I hadn't done midwifery when Bea was pregnant. It was too close for comfort and I might have made a few wrong assumptions about her condition. I think that's why lots of doctors refuse to treat their own families, apart from it being considered unethical.'

Paul grinned. 'It took Aunt Emily thirty seconds to diagnose Sadie, and the same with Bea.'

Emma shrugged. 'Nothing in her witch's mind for me yet, but she didn't say we would never have a baby and you know how frank she is as a rule.'

'Cheer up, you look pensive. Even Emily gets it wrong sometimes, or her timing is wrong.'

'Not often! I was thinking of something we talked about. She has had dreams about my mother.'

'You've done what you can to keep in touch, but your mother is a very hard woman, and I can't suggest what more you could do, as she never answers your letters.'

'Aunt Emily is going to write to her doctor and her solicitor in case she is ever ill and needs help. I thought about it and if she was really ill, I couldn't go there to look after her in that miserable house. If it came to the crunch we'd have to take her in here.'

'That's what I said long ago, Darling. I agree that it would be impossible for you to go back and relive some of the unhappy things that happened there.'

Emma sighed. 'I had a very happy time working in Bristol but that house was deadly. As soon as I entered the front door I felt depressed. It was completely empty of love. Hold me, Paul. I feel cold. For years I thought all families were like mine and it was a revelation to go into another home and find warmth and affection that wasn't just for show when visitors came.'

'We may not have Bea and Aunt Emily here for Christmas but I'm looking forward to seeing a few old friends and we can take time off for ourselves for a change.'

'I'd like that, but if there are a few people who have nowhere to go in their off duty at St Thomas's they can come here. Travelling isn't easy and a meal and a warm fire might appeal.' She saw his doubts and laughed. 'Bea as usual has been busy. We had a parcel from the General today. Just because he is Dwight's godfather means that she bosses him as she does everybody and told him that we might starve if we didn't have a little Christmas cheer. There is a turkey in the fridge and a pile of canned food and you'd be doing me a favour if you bring in a few people to eat it all.'

'I'll scour the highways.' Paul knew that

she missed Bea and her family on the Island and that she needed a few new faces to take away her underlying sadness.

From the past a voice came to Emma. She saw again the cold blue eyes of Sister Cary, the harsh woman in the first nursing situation in which Emma found herself so many years ago. It was the morning after a bad raid and Emma's best friend, a vibrant Welsh girl, had been killed and Emma was prostrated with grief. 'Work and more work is the remedy for grief,' Sister Cary had said. 'I know all about that. I lost my fiancé in the first lot.'

I am a happy married woman with a very interesting life, so I have no right to feel deprived and sad. Sister Cary was right. Work smoothes out the creases and if I can never have a child, I must endure it.

'I'll make sure the spare beds are made up,' she said. 'We can take four or five guests over the Christmas period.'

'Isn't that too much hard work?'

'Mick will help and if we have no patients at that time, I can do the cooking and Eileen can take it easy. Honestly, I shall enjoy it and I might ask Esme Bolt from Casualty at Beatties as she will be alone in her off duty. Her family were

89

killed and she no longer has roots in her home town as it was a place that was devastated. She lost everyone.'

'We're apt to forget that there are so many lonely, bereaved people now,' he agreed. 'Just don't start a charity for the lost and homeless, that's all!'

'I know that there will be some who are on duty over Christmas but a lot of patients who can be discharged over the holiday like to go home and the local Society of Jewish Women step in to help out, as Christmas is not their festival. They enjoy helping as they feel grateful to Beatties for what the hospital has done for their families over the years.'

Paul picked up the phone. 'I'll ring Gordon at Tommie's. It's good to know that some people still help in a practical way and are allowed to do so. It's a pity about some well-established charitable groups. With the New Health Service, everything isn't as yet all sweetness and light. There's a lot of wastage that I'm sure the country can't afford.'

Emma nodded agreement. 'The local ladies, mostly ex-patients who came in each week and helped with the linen and the mending and making swabs at

Beatties, have been told that the State will now supply labour for that and they are no longer needed. It's a bitter blow to simple women who like to feel important in a small way, to put on a white coat and cap and sit with others, chatting and doing a lot of valuable work. It's a slap in the face for people who *need* to serve in some small way, and many found it very therapeutic and good for fighting depression.'

'On another level,' Paul added, 'I was talking to one of our leading consultants who does a lot of hospital work, incidentally, more than he need do, apart from his own private cases. Cecil said, "I have a good typist and a boy who tidies the office and my private consulting rooms and he takes messages. My wife answers the phone if she's at home and everything gets done quickly and efficiently. I hardly ever mislay notes and I know my patients. Now they tell me that as I am so high up in the pecking order, I am due for and I *must have* two secretaries and another typist. What am I going to do with them? They'll sit there knitting and get fat and lazy and nobody will be responsible for anything."' Paul laughed 'Cecil says he'll use one for pleasure and choose a really gorgeous piece, but I think he's joking! Have you seen his wife? She'd kill him! His wife says she'll choose his new staff and anyone with legs can forget it.'

'Is that Cecil Tasker?' Emma giggled. 'He does like nice legs. He grumbled in theatre when we wore sloppy gowns that reached the floor. Nobody took any notice as he's not attractive and knows it. He sweats a lot when operating, but at least has a sense of humour and means no harm. I was quite fond of him. He's a very good surgeon and cares about his patients. I'd forgotten he did cases at Tommie's too.'

'Mostly private there but takes a few clinics when we need help, but who knows, if demarcation of work is enforced in surgery and clinics, they'll lose a lot of willing and valuable help.'

## Chapter Five

'It's all glitter, baubles and false snow in Washington.' Bea's voice was clear over the transatlantic telephone line and to Emma it seemed as if she was in the house.

92

'It must look wonderful.' She sounded wistful.

'Phoney! Even the boughs of holly and mistletoe in our porch are fake. I bet you have lots of fresh holly with the berries dropping off in an irritating way and squashed mistletoe berries underfoot and the smell of fir trees, and bands of faded paper streamers and real Christmas. If I hear 'Jingle Bells' once more from some old street organ cranked up by a wino, I'll throw up.'

'That sounds like my best friend,' Emma stated mildly.

'Thank God for that.'

'For what?'

'For being my best friend. I know I'm the luckiest woman alive to have Dwight and the twins all bursting with health, so don't go on to me, but I never thought I'd miss England so much. It's a real pain and Dwight says I'm a pain too, so I must be a bit mad.'

'You'll have a wonderful time.' Emma tried to sound soothing, then in a burst of candour, 'You *are* lucky; luckier than you'll ever know! I envy you so much having the twins, that I ache inside.'

'Emma? You are crying!' Bea's voice

came down an octave and she was all warmth and concern. 'Damn this phone and damn the wide Atlantic. I should be there. I knew this morning I ought to be with you and thought it was just my own selfish bloody-mindedness. What happened?'

'Nothing. That's the point.'

'Not a miscarriage?'

'Nothing got that far and nothing will.'

'Tell Auntie all about it.'

Bea listened while Emma spelled out her visit to the obstetrician and she found a blessed release in talking to her.

'I know at least two people who had their tubes inflated and both gave birth successfully a little later.'

'She did say that she thought it would happen,' Emma admitted, 'But Eileen is pregnant after all this time and I think I'm feeling jealous and sorry for myself but I daren't show it.'

'I think the recipe is to forget it for a while and go for other things but I know how really hard that can be. When Dwight was unable and I found that I had to read in bed and wear nice little nighties *all* night, I decided that we could never have a family and I felt as you do, but you have

Paul and the clinic and lots of friends and the possibility of it coming right in time.'

'I know all that.'

'And I sound like an agony aunt who has no idea about life! Doesn't help, does it?'

'It helps. It's just that Christmas should be special and I do miss you all. Feel better now, thank you Ma'am! At least Aunt Emily hasn't told me that I shall be barren all my life! She is much more concerned that I don't upset George, who is staying there with the rest of them for Christmas and he thought that Paul and I would be there.'

'Tricky.'

'So she says but I think we could be friends.'

'Forget it! I think that George will love you for ever but he must have space to find another woman. By the way, your parcels arrived safely thanks to Dwight's contact who flew them over and delivered them by hand—then looked pathetic, so that's one more we have here for Christmas, as the poor man was without bed or board and had done us a real favour, yes sir!'

'You'll love it and in a way, so will I. We have a lot of parties lined up with the medics and we've invited a few to stay.

Tell Dwight that his godfather came up trumps again and we have food galore.'

'So we are both going to have a ball, as they say here?'

'It seems so.'

'Dwight is making noises like a peevish goat and saying that there are a few million other people waiting to use the lines and say Happy Christmas, so I'll let him say his bit and I'll say *courage mon enfant* and have a good time.'

'How is Bea? I thought she was good for you just now.'

'Have you noticed, Paul, that when she needs help or encouragement, I am strong and when I need it, she's the same?'

'It's like that for us, too.'

'But with us it's one-sided. You are always the strong one.'

'Don't you believe it! I'd never have had the courage to start up here without your full support.'

She kissed him and smiled. 'Let's go on believing we are both wonderful. Now where did I leave my lists? If you don't need me, I ought to sort out the beds as they will be here this evening, probably all at once. Mick has done the bed-pushing and cleaned the bathrooms and I have put the turkey giblets to cook slowly with vegetables and herbs for giblet soup tonight. Some of the cheeses and fruit that the General sent will do for afters and Eileen feels fine today so is able to make a lot of soda bread and Scotch pancakes and we have masses of butter from Aunt Emily. I hope they don't notice that we have no homemade Christmas cake as Eileen ate it all. We'll have to put up with American angel cake and a Victoria sponge.'

'Do you want to go to midnight service?'

'No, Paul. I vowed never to go again on Christmas Eve. Bea and I found it much too heart-rending as it brought back such poignant memories.'

'Good. Tonight I can keep a dry hankie. We'll stay and give the returning worshippers a wassail bowl. It will have to be cider and roasted apples and cloves and a little brandy, but it will save our precious coffee for tomorrow.'

'Bea feels the same about Christmas Eve. On the phone she admitted that she couldn't cope with it in a church service but she feels as if she is a big fraud. She kindly suggested that her nanny and helpers should have Christmas Eve off duty and she will look after the twins and the guests while they have a good time. They think she's 'jus wunnerful' and unselfish but we know better.'

The telephone seemed busier than even on the fullest working day and Emma was touched to know that so many people rang to wish them well. Aunt Janey seemed excited and told her that they'd managed to find a box of old decorations and a tiny doll that she'd dressed in pink silk for the top of the Christmas tree, and Clive was busily trying to open parcels he'd found in a cupboard that were intended for the next morning. Emily said all was well and George was out with Wilf fetching more wood for the fires.

'Is that why you rang now?' Emma asked dryly.

'He got over his first disappointment when he found that you wouldn't be here, called me a conniving witch and managed to find it funny, so that's another hurdle over. Clive doesn't give him much time to brood about you, Sadie or the situation in Korea so we might have quite a nice time. I'll say that you and Paul sent your best and keep him busy until he goes back in three days' time.'

'After that I suppose I dare show my face on the Island again?'

'As soon as you like. Goodbye for now. I hear voices and I want you off the line.'

'Give George my love.'

'Cheeky monkey! I'll do no such thing.'

'Who now?' Emma came back to the telephone as it rang again before she reached the office door. This was becoming a time waster in the nicest possible way, and Paul wanted to use the phone to ring people in Bristol when there was a gap, but there were a lot of things to be done before the guests arrived. In a weak moment she'd told them to come early and have tea but now she wished she'd put the time later.

Abruptly, she lifted the receiver and recited the telephone number. There was silence except for a faint background of voices and a slight gasp as if the caller had found the wrong number, and when Emma repeated it, the line went dead.

'Use the phone now before it rings again,' Emma suggested to Paul. 'We are now getting wrong numbers which we certainly don't need.'

'I'll ring Bristol and after that you can

ignore any more calls as I shall be here for a while, but if there's one for you, I'll call you on the house phone and you can come back and get it here.'

'Thank you. I do have a lot to do. Send my love to anyone you think deserves it and put off anyone else who wants to have food and bed. I feel as if we are opening a ward, not just having people here for Christmas. Who *is* Robert Grover? He's downstairs now, chatting to Eileen while she makes bread.'

'My fault. He was a house surgeon in Bristol and a good friend. He put me up in his very small flat when I was desperate for digs and I owe him.' Paul began to dial and while the ringing tone began, he grinned.

'Tell Eileen to be careful. He's a bit of a lad with the girls.'

'Tell Eileen? What about me? Don't you think he'll fancy me?'

'I'm bigger than Robert. He wouldn't dare.' He waved her away. 'Hello, is Dr Grey there?'

Emma was still smiling when she went down to the main kitchen and found Eileen blushing in a rather complacent way at something that Robert was saying.

'Oh, there you are, Robert. Paul has been putting me in the picture. Now I know all about you.'

'Everything?' He tried to sound alarmed but laughed.

'How are you getting on, Eileen? It all looks and smells wonderful.' Emma smiled at the good-looking man. 'You are much too big to be ornamental so make yourself useful and stir the soup.'

'I might have known that Paul would marry a hospital Sister! I've seen that look many times and I always obey. What's that in the bowl? I think I'd rather stir that, and don't you think it needs tasting?'

'No, that's our wassail bowl for later. You shall have some when Paul finishes in the office and the others arrive.'

'Who will be here? Anyone I know?' Robert stirred the thick vegetable and giblet soup and took a deeply sentimental breath. 'I haven't smelled this for years. My granny used to make it for us. Before she was bombed,' he added sadly with a sideways glance at Eileen who looked dangerously sympathetic.

'You're in good company. We all know about bombs, don't we, Love?' Mick stood in the doorway and grinned. 'I thought I knew all the chat-up lines but that's a good one.'

'Who is this?' Robert asked with mock horror.

'I'm her bloke, I live here and I cope with difficult patients, do some book work and make a good chucker-out when necessary.' Mick's laugh hid a glint of steel.

'And he's our good friend and helper, Mick Grade,' Emma said warmly.

'Wish I'd never been born!'

'Is Sister Devon coming?' Mick asked. Emma nodded. 'Now she's more your cup of tea, squire. Lots of glamour, no commitments, and she's not pregnant like Eileen here. Want a beer, Mate? I could do with one, myself.' They all relaxed and Eileen went to put her feet up for an hour, at Emma's insistence.

'You'll be up late tonight and even if your sickness is much less now, you must take care.'

'Thanks Sister,' Mick said and she knew that he wanted Eileen away from the charismatic doctor.

Paul came into the room, took the teapot and shook it. 'I think that's all my calls. I couldn't get two of them but they may be away with their families. Can we spare a fresh pot?'

'I brought some tea,' Robert said. 'I know that nurses drink it all the time as a substitute for the milk of human kindness.'

'You've put him in his place?' Paul asked mildly. 'That saves a lot of trouble. Most of the men steer him away from their womenfolk, but I knew you could cope with him.'

'You should have seen Sister and her friend Bea sort out the rough ones in hospital. Enough to make a man's ...'

'Yes, we know, Mick,' Paul interrupted. 'By the way, when I was looking up a phone number, a call came and when I answered it, a female voice asked if I was Mick Grade, then obviously realised she didn't recognise the voice and said sorry, and rang off.'

'Aha! The other woman,' Robert said maliciously.

'Didn't she say anything?' Mick seemed puzzled. 'What kind of voice?'

Paul shrugged. 'Ordinary. London accent, I think, but it was only a few words.'

'Was there any background noise?' Emma asked.

'Not a lot. Just a vague distant muddle of voices as if she rang from a public place, a hotel or a bar.'

'Funny. I answered a call that had that sound in the background but whoever it was rang off as soon as I said our number.'

'It wasn't you she wanted, only your wonderful Mick,' Robert teased.

'Well, I don't know any women except my sister Myra,' Mick ventured, 'but she doesn't live in London now. Come to think of it, I don't know where she lives. We never got on. She married a Canadian during the war but he was killed, so she has a pension and needs nothing from me.'

'Maybe she heard that you lived here and wanted to wish you a Merry Christmas,' Paul suggested.

'Unlikely,' Mick replied. 'Do you want any more apples roasted for the punch? We're going to need a lot as you seem to have invited the whole of London!'

'I also brought a bottle of brandy and some spices,' Robert said modestly. 'I was going to suggest a hot beverage of sorts but I see it is already in hand.'

'All we need is brandy and spices,' Mick said. 'But you needn't think that

Eileen will drink too much and tell you the story of her life as she is off booze for the duration of the pregnancy and will have to stay sober.'

'I'll make do with Sister Devon.'

'Telephone,' Emma said. 'Why don't you answer it in case it's your mystery caller, Mick.'

He hesitated, then nodded and made for the office, raised the receiver and said the number of the clinic.

'Mick, is that you?'

'Who is this?'

She laughed. 'Your sister Myra, silly. I've been trying to get you all day, off and on.'

'What do you want?'

'Is that the way to talk to me? With Christmas and all. It's been a long time, Mick.'

'What do you want?' He repeated.

'Just to say hello.'

'Hello.'

'I heard you lived in and had a nice cushy number.'

'Who said?'

'I met one of your oppos in the pub.'

'Where?'

'I work in a pub near the Elephant.'

'The Elephant and Castle in London?'

'Don't sound so surprised. It's not bad as jobs go but I wanted a change and wondered if there was a place for me with you.' He said nothing and she put on a pleading tone. 'I've been poorly, Mick. I feel rotten and I want to come to stay with you for a few days even if I can't work there. Bert said it's a big house with plenty of room. I could do the cleaning and such. Doctor's place, isn't it?'

Mick silently cursed his too voluble friend and sent his soul to hell.

'Well, cat got your tongue?'

'It's *no,* Myra. I wouldn't have you here for all the tea in China. Clean? You couldn't clean a doorstep, let alone a house, and we have all the staff we need.'

'No need to get shirty! I may come round and talk to the doctor.' Her voice was shrill and resentful. 'It's all right for some. You seem to have landed on your feet and you always did get the best of things, but I lost my husband and I am lonely.'

'Keep away, Myra,' he warned.

'I'll ask your doctor. He had a nice voice on the phone. I think he'd be a bit more sympathetic than my own brother. He may offer me a job.'

'Don't try it, Myra. Stick to what suits you, serving behind a bar in a rough pub.'

'I have to go as it's getting busy. See you after Christmas when it's not so busy. TTFN.'

'Ta Ta For Now? No! I don't want to see you.' Mick looked down at the now silent phone and with a sinking feeling recalled that Myra had always been a troublemaker and hung on to what she wanted to do regardless of other people.

'A problem?' Mick turned to Paul who lounged in the doorway.

'Could be, but I don't want to worry you with it.'

'You live here, Mick. If you are upset it reflects on all of us.'

'My sister Myra says she might turn up here and ask you for a job. I told her it would be impossible. I hate to say this but my sister is a slut and the last person I want Eileen to meet, especially now.'

'Tell me about her.'

Mick calmed down and after a few minutes, Paul nodded. 'I get the picture. Even if she was a good worker we'd have no vacancy here and you couldn't put her up in your flat when the baby arrives.'

'She doesn't know about the flat or the baby. She thinks that Eileen and me live-in here.'

'If she rings again don't enlighten her about that as she might arrive on your own doorstep with bag and baggage. You could hint that you have only one room here but might have to find other accommodation if we take in patients.'

Mick blenched visibly. 'Crikey. If she saw our nice flat, that would set the cat among the pigeons!'

'Exactly. If she comes here, leave her to me. Now get down to the kitchen and start moving chairs into the dining room.'

'We aren't going to take in patients are we Doc?'

'I hope not.' Paul looked reassuring. 'It's not what I want to do, but the hint might be enough to put off any person not familiar with disturbed people.'

Paul made a note of Myra's married name and told Emma of his conversation with Mick.

'She will be busy over Christmas and Boxing Day in the pub,' Emma surmised. 'But the day after that might be the time when she could come here. I'll tell Mrs Coster to look out for her and ring you on the house phone if she sees her.'

'Mrs Coster will love that,' Paul said dryly. 'It's strange how clean our front hall tiles are when we expect patients or visitors!'

Mick came back to the office to tell them that all the guests were now in the drawing room. 'Had an accident with the bunch of mistletoe in the kitchen,' he said mildly.

'It was the only piece I could get from a market trader,' Emma said. 'No Christmas kissing?'

'Not if I have anything to do with it. That Doctor can find his own. Not that he needs it with Sister Devon, but he's not getting up to any shenanigans with my Eileen.'

'Tell him he has to be sober enough to carve the turkey tomorrow. He gets that job as he's a budding surgeon,' Paul said. 'Cheer up Mick. It may never happen,' he called to his retreating back.

'I thought you hated clichés.' Emma laughed.

'If I'm with Mick for more than a few minutes, I copy him. It's catching.'

'I hope that's all that is.'

'Why? Is there a bug going round?'

Emma shrugged. 'Not that I have heard, but if there is, Mrs Coster will know at least five families who have caught it! I think her own family have formed their own immunity as they seldom have anything wrong. She said they all had the usual things as infants, and to use her expression, "I bunged them all in together to get it over in one go when they had measles and such," and it seemed to have worked for her.'

'She didn't know how wise she was,' Paul said. 'That is taught now as the best way with certain infectious diseases so that they don't catch them when they grow up and become adults. They are often much more ill if they have it later in life. Take German measles for instance. It doesn't make the child very ill but they have spots and feel off colour before the spots come out. If a pregnant woman catches it in early pregnancy, the baby can develop badly and have a lot of rather nasty problems like blindness, deafness or even heart disease and death.'

'Eileen mentioned that the Sister in antenatal warned them to keep away from any children with infectious diseases until they are over the third month, but we don't have children here as patients very often and they need never meet Eileen.'

'Put the office light out and close the door. Any calls now can be ignored. I am not expecting a patient and at least with this work I seldom get emergencies, so forget everything but Christmas and friends and very good food ... and us. That's all that matters.'

## Chapter Six

'Not even enough turkey left to make rissoles, but we can open a few tins of sausages and bacon that the General sent with the other things.' Emma opened the store cupboard and pursed her lips.

Eileen looked at the scraped bare carcass of what had been a huge bird, and dumped it in the waste bin. 'I feel all right now after the sickness earlier this morning. I can make pastry with all that lovely fat they pack round the sausages. I'll say this for the Yanks, they put nice things in cans. You'll enjoy a nice pie, Sister.'

'Make enough for us all. I know we agreed that you would cater for yourselves but this is a special time and we share everything until the New Year and then go back to rations.'

'You say that all the time, but you give us lots of nice things,' Eileen remarked.

'You need good food now,' Emma said lightly and found that she was able to regard Eileen's pregnancy with easy objectivity. The girl's skin was clear and her eyes sparkled. 'Is that skirt getting tight?

'Not from the baby, that's too early, but Mick said I'm a greedy guts and ate far too much over Christmas, and so I did.' She chuckled. 'It was really nice, Sister. Everyone was friendly and Mick and I had a good time as they all helped with the washing-up and the bed-making.'

'It went very well,' Emma agreed. 'We haven't left too much mess for Mrs Coster to clean, except for the front hall. That had a lot of mud trampled in but she will be only too eager to scrub the tiles once I tell her to watch out for an unwelcome visitor we are expecting.'

'You mean Mick's sister?' Eileen looked worried. 'I shall keep out of the way unless Dr Paul wants me in the consulting room to chaperone someone, but really, I'm dying to see what she looks like. Mick won't let me meet her as he says that Myra has always been bad news. I've never seen him so set against anyone as he is with her.'

It was odd how the phonecall from Mick's sister had made an impact on them all and Mick went about his duties with a set face and hard eyes, as if he was ready to fight any attempt to upset his life with Eileen and the couple who were so good to them. Emma had a definite sense of misgiving, even though it was unlikely that Myra could alter the happy state of the household in Kensington.

Even Paul seemed concerned.

'Mick and Eileen would be irreplaceable,' he said when Emma remarked that he seemed pensive. 'Mick said that if she gives trouble, he will have to leave and take a job up north, and he sounded as if he was adamant.'

'This can't affect them too much. We only have to tell her to go away and she'll see that she isn't welcome. We have the right to refuse to let her past the front door. Surely she can't be the monster that Mick thinks her to be? It isn't as if she is in real need of work. She told Mick that she has a job and lives in at the pub so he has no need to feel guilty about her.'

'If she comes here today, she'll be here after lunch, mid-afternoon.' Paul said.

'How do you know that?'

'Licensing hours. They will need her in the mornings and evenings but the pubs shut all the afternoon. That's when barmaids are likely to be off-duty. There are buses from the Elephant and Castle to bring her to the West End, but she'd have to change at Victoria I think, and might have a fairly long walk if the transport is bad, so she will have to be very determined see Mick if she goes to all that effort.'

'You have it worked out?'

'No, that was Mick. He wants the cannons primed to shoot her on sight!'

'We don't want unpleasantness if there are patients booked for the afternoon!'

'I've told Mick to stay away from the hall and Mrs Coster will keep her there until I get downstairs. She will adore being a detective, looking out for her arrival. All I hope is that she doesn't get too officious and give her a piece of her mind before Myra has a chance to say a word and I am not there, but even if she seems less of a threat than we have been led to believe from Mick's colourful desription of her, we need Mick and Eileen so what we think of her will not matter. We are selfishly prejudiced in their favour.'

'You'd better slide down the bannisters to get down to the hall quickly! I'll try to be available too.'

Lunch was a quiet affair and Emma ate her soup and bread slowly, the aura of expectant concern being almost tangible as she imagined the house without Mick and Eileen. She'd miss the birth of the baby and Eileen would be lonely if they had to start life again in an area that was unfamiliar. Myra must be very objectionable if she made Mick consider such a radical solution as leaving London to be rid of her.

The smell of pies filtered through and she hoped that their evening dinner cooking didn't make the house seem too homely and inviting. She closed the kitchen door. The odour of the strong disinfectant that Mrs Coster thought was essential to cleaning the house wafted up the stairs and blotted out the more pleasant aromas.

'Two patients today,' Paul said. 'Eileen will be needed for one and she might as well stay for the other, if I am called away. She chats to them while they wait for me when I am called to the phone and they like her. She can stay in the office until I need her.'

'It's nothing to do with us, but I do feel edgy,' Emma admitted. 'Mick and Eileen have come to mean a lot here in so many ways and I hate seeing them unhappy.'

'Just be there when she comes but leave me to talk to her. We may need you to keep Mrs Coster in order. I wish I'd never mentioned Myra to her but I had to have warning so that we could keep her in the hall and let her come in no further.'

Emma tidied the medicine cupboard and checked that Paul had all he needed for emergencies, and enough stock to dispense his own prescriptions. Over the past few months the stocks had increased and she saw that he had prepared a few bottles and pill-boxes ready for the patients on his next appointment lists, but it was becoming more common for patients to have to collect medicines from a chemist, after handing in prescriptions from their doctors. She remembered the stiff white paper wrappings, sealed with red sealing wax on bottles that she had collected from the surgery as a child. It had been impressive even if the mixture was only white medicine for heartburn.

Faintly, she heard the front door bell and went to the head of the stairs. Mrs Coster answered the door and stood back as one of Paul's regular patients asked for his prescribed medicines and left as soon as Paul saw him briefly in the clinic. Mrs Coster washed the same tiles for the third time, their colours vivid against the grimy ones as yet untouched by scrubbing brush or soap and when the bell sounded again, she rubbed her hands nearly dry on her sacking apron and went to the door.

The young woman standing there had a look of defiance mixed with apprehension. She wrinkled her nose as the smell of disinfectant met her from Mrs Coster's bucket and she hesitated.

'Yes?' Mrs Coster said in a very off-putting tone. She had noticed with one glance the cheapness of the brightly coloured coat, the unpolished shoes and the fact that she had seen similar hats on the bargain counter of the Bon Marche in Brixton. She decided the girl needed a good wash and all her watchdog instincts surfaced. 'What do you want?'

'I want to see the doctor.'

'What time are you booked to see him? He's a very busy man and you need an appointment.'

Myra resented being talked to in such a patronising manner by someone she recognised as from her own background. 'Don't you talk to me like that! You are only the cleaner. It's nothing to do with you why I'm here. I want to see the doctor.'

'What name shall I say?' Mrs Coster pointed to a bench just inside the door. 'Wipe your feet and sit there.' She raised the house phone and Paul answered quickly. The front door bell rang again and Mrs Coster went to open it and in passing Myra said, 'The doctor is expecting a patient who has an appointment and he's on his way down, so sit there and be quiet until he can see you.'

Paul crossed the hall as a distraught woman swept past Mrs Coster. 'Mrs Donoghue? Where is Maurice?'

'I left him with his brother in the car so that I could talk to you. He's calm now but last night none of us slept as he was throwing things around in his room and he struck the maid when she took in some tea this morning. He said she wanted to poison him and his voices have started telling him things again.'

'Is he taking his medicine?'

She shook her head. 'He said he was but he admitted last night that he disliked what it did to him and he'd tipped the whole bottle of tablets down the sink a few days ago.'

'This is serious. I think he needs sedation and hospital treatment. Bring him up to the clinic and I'll give him something to calm him before he is admitted.'

Myra shrank back as if she wanted to merge with the wallpaper as a pale-faced, wild-eyed youth was led in by a slightly older man. Emma appeared and smiled. 'Hello Maurice. Come upstairs, it's warmer there.'

He nodded and followed her obediently with his family and Paul turned to Myra, who by now appeared to be really frightened. 'I hear from Mick Grade that you would like to work here.'

'No, I just wanted to see him, in case he could put me up for a few days,' she muttered hastily and backed away. 'It doesn't matter. I'll be off now.'

'I'm afraid he's not here at the moment.

He does work for me sometimes but doesn't actually live in this house. He has lodgings nearby but is thinking of leaving for a job in the north.' Paul smiled in a friendly way. 'If you need a job, we might be able to use you if you like the work, but you don't seem very strong.' His voice was calm but she seemed scared and his words added nothing to her comfort. 'There's a spare room but I'm afraid it's next to the clinic and is sometimes noisy.'

Myra gave a stifled cry and shook her head.

'You seem worried. Have I got it wrong? Did you want to see me as a doctor for another matter?' he remarked, as if she might have another reason for coming to the house.

'She needs a doctor but not your sort. Look at her! She's got a nerve, coming here covered in spots!' Mrs Coster was indignant, and Paul took a closer look at the woman whose face was covered with cosmetic powder which didn't hide the pin-point spots.

'It's only a rash,' Myra said defensively. 'They've all had it at the pub.'

'I've brought up five children and they all had that at the same time. It's German measles isn't it, Doctor?' Mrs Coster diagnosed with triumph.

'I'm sorry I can't help you. I'm not that kind of medic. I don't treat infectious diseases, I deal with the mind and nervous disorders.'

'You run a loony bin!' Myra said accusingly. 'If you think I'd want to work here you must be mad too.' She glanced apprehensively up the wide stairs as a muted crash from the consulting room indicated something broken, and she made for the door. 'You can keep your job. Don't wonder Mick sleeps out! You need a warder, not a helper. Me have a room in this house and a room next door to all that into the bargain? I'd be murdered in my bed.'

Emma saw Eileen peering between the bannister rails, one foot on the first stair as if on her way down to the hall, obviously fascinated by the scene below. She wanted to shout, 'Go back', but knew she must be quiet and not alert Myra to Eileen's presence. She was determined that they must have no physical contact. She sprinted up the stairs and seized the puzzled young woman by one arm, pushing her back into the office. 'Stay there,' she whispered. 'Stay there until I come for you and don't move!'

'I only wanted to see her,' Eileen protested in an aggrieved tone and Myra glanced up when she heard the short scuffle that ensued.

'I suppose that's another one that wants locking up,' Myra said and sneered. 'Regular asylum you've got here. I'd never feel safe in this house and I wouldn't come here if you begged me to take a job, not for ten pounds a week!'

'I'm not offering you a job,' Paul said. 'I think you'd be unsuitable for my patients. Do you want to leave a message for Mick. He might be here later.'

'Just tell him I'm going to Canada. I wanted to stay in England but my husband's family sent me some money and said I'd be welcome so I'm going next week. I just thought that Mick might help me instead. I'd rather stay here in England.'

'There seems to be nothing here for you,' Paul said firmly. 'Mick has his own life to lead and his own job to do and I think you'll like Canada. Is there work for you where you are going?'

She bit her lip. 'I wanted to get away

from bar work but I suppose as Mick said, that's all I'm fit for. They own a hotel and I shall have to work there unless I find a nice chap and get married again.' She added, her eyes holding a predatory gleam, 'Canadians like British women.'

Emma called from the upper landing. 'Dr Sykes, will you please come up here at once?'

Mrs Coster opened the front door wide and jerked her head in the direction of the front garden. 'Mind the step. We don't want you laid up here with a sprained ankle!'

'I'm going. This place gives me the creeps.' Myra slammed the door after her and Paul gave a sigh of relief.

'Could you sponge the bench and anything she touched? Eileen must not catch German measles just now. It's very important.'

'She'll not come back. Wanted something for nothing if you ask me, but she's scared of anyone a bit off their trolley.'

What would my patients think if they heard that? he wondered wryly, and went up to give Maurice an injection before the ambulance came to take him to a secure hospital where he would have sympathetic treatment for schizophrenia.

'Sorry about the crash,' Emma said. 'The wind took a vase off the top of the tallboy, but it wasn't a good one that we'll miss.' She lowered her voice and stood away from the couch where Maurice lay with his eyes closed. 'I think he acted up at home because he thought you'd let him stay here, but I told him we don't take in-patients and he seems resigned to it now.'

'He still needs sedation. He hasn't been taking his medication and he might be unpredictable. Go and say nice things to Eileen. I think she's crying in the office!'

Emma was contrite. 'I'm sorry I was a bit rough just now Eileen. Why don't you go for a rest?' she suggested. 'Tell Mick he can come out. The enemy has retreated.'

Eileen dried her eyes but still looked unhappy. 'You frightened me.'

'I had to push you into the office as Myra has German measles and you must not touch anyone with it now that you are expecting. The baby is worth more than the push I gave you. I'll tell you all about it later, but make up your mind that for the next few weeks you must not go into crowded places, and the cinema will be out of bounds. Sorry about it but I know that Mick will see the dangers and insist on it.' She smiled. 'We all have an interest in your health.'

Eileen laughed shakily. 'I should have done as I was told and stayed out of sight but I heard voices and thought she'd not see if I peeped over at her. I thought German measles was nothing much. I didn't have it but some of my friends at school did and they didn't seem very ill.'

'That's true, unless a pregnant woman catches it and then the baby might be born with something wrong, so you can see that I was worried about you.'

'Have you had it, Sister?'

'Yes, I think so and it wouldn't matter if I caught it now, as I am not pregnant.'

Emma and Mrs Coster dragged the damp bench out of the hall and left it in the porch to dry and lose the pungent smell of antiseptic that Mrs Coster imagined would kill any germ that it touched, but her scrubbing had done nothing for the pattern of the fabric covering.

'Well done,' Emma praised her weakly and left her to finish the hall and to make up a highly coloured account of what she had witnessed that afternoon so that she could tell her family when she left work.

'I feel like celebrating,' Mick said when Eileen found him and he was convinced that Myra had gone for good. 'Heaven help the Canadians! Myra can be soft as a kitten when it comes to men, until she has them in her nasty hot hands and then she shows what she's really like and takes them to the cleaners. The man she married was killed while he was still keen and in the honeymoon period and so his family must think she's OK.'

'We can't celebrate,' Eileen said. 'No cinema for weeks and weeks and I wanted to see Dorothy Lamour at the Gaumont.'

'We'll go a lot when the doc says it's safe,' Mick promised her. 'But Mrs Coster said that there's a lot of illness among the market people and even her family are a bit careful now.'

'Out-patients at Tommie's is busy,' Paul remarked. 'A lot of men from the Forces came out with TB and anaemia and they are paying the price of bad food and lack of fresh air now. Submariners are the worst. Imagine being shut up for days on end in a metal box, breathing in everyone's germs and eating basic rations.

Some were not diagnosed as the first symptoms were slight, but now they are being treated seriously. It's such a relief to know they have the chance of being cured with streptomycin instead of having to spend months in a sanitorium. They also have a lot of returned prisoners of war suffering from malnutrition and psychiatric conditions. I have a fair share of those in my clinics.'

'The new health service seems to be working, but many people go to surgeries for the slightest thing now that they pay nothing. Aunt Emily says that the surgery down there is full every day and she has to be firm with some of the people who obviously only need an aspirin but demand to see the doctor.'

Paul laughed. 'And as she probably knew their parents and saw them as babies, they are more frightened of her than of the doctor, but he knows her judgement is good.'

'I think that George leaves today for Scotland, and Aunt Janey and the others go back to the mainland too. Maybe I'll telephone tomorrow when Aunt Emily has had time to recover from an active baby and a houseful of guests.'

'Very wise.' Paul's eyes were full of understanding. 'I have every sympathy with George. What would I do without you?'

'He has Clive.'

'Don't be sad. Time is on our side and as you've said, they've shaken the tree and there's a better chance now, so who knows, when the fruit is ready, we may be lucky and it will be worth waiting for. Before that we have a lot to do here. Several of the rooms need papering and you said that Eileen wanted to renovate curtains when she can't do other work, so that needs organising.'

Emma laughed. 'There's no need to worry that I shall be bored and doleful. I love it here and wouldn't change a thing ... except the wallpaper, but I think that the designs available are very limited and the quality is poor. The old wallpaper looks better, even in the bedrooms. The alternative is that stuff I hate, the coarse paper with raised pattern that needs distempering once it's hung and makes for double the work. It never looks more than café wallpaper.'

'We'll leave the walls alone for a while then,' Paul agreed.

Emma checked the rooms for cleaning

and lingered in the light airy room that had been a nursery; not the one that Bea used, but the one with a linen cupboard still smelling faintly of lavender and the remains of the frieze of small animals and nursery rhyme characters. She closed the door softly. That must stay as it was until it could be used for the purpose for which it was meant, if that was possible. She shook away her sudden depression. One baby in the house would do for the near future.

The small pile of Christmas cards that had had to wait until the guests had gone and Emma had time to read them, now filled a pleasant half-hour while she drank a cup of tea.

She curled up on the settee in the drawing room and smiled softly when she saw that so many people still remembered her and Paul. She shook her head over the one that George sent with his usual cryptic message, 'Love you 'til Hell freezes', and she was slightly bemused by one from an old patient whom she had nursed during her brief period of private nursing. 'I wonder how he knew where to find me?' she asked Paul.

'He's the type to keep tabs on anyone

who interests him,' Paul replied. 'A phone-call to Beatties probably did the trick.' She read the message again from the titled man she'd refused to marry, knowing that he wanted her because their close association as Nursing Sister and patient made him confuse love with caring gratitude. She also knew that their lifestyles would never match and so she had made it possible for him to marry a county girl from a neighbouring estate who would ride with him, entertain important people and give him a large family ... and get along with his domineering mother, she added to herself.

'Thank you, my dear wise Emma,' he wrote in his card. 'You were right and I have found happiness again, but I shall never forget your sweet face and kindness.'

Tears blurred her eyes. Such a proud man and one that any woman might love, but not for her.

Paul stretched contentedly. 'I hid some coffee beans from the ravening hordes and I think we deserve some now. I'll grind the beans and make it.' He smiled at her. 'It's been a good Christmas on the whole.'

'Different and interesting,' she agreed. 'Who needs Santa Claus?'

# Chapter Seven

Emma arranged dark green leaves from the flourishing castor oil plant that seemed to thrive even in the poor soil by the back door, putting them in a white vase on a table against the crimson curtains in the hall. It was the best she could do as there was nothing in the barren garden to add colour and she knew that the flowers from the stall across the park would fade in a day or so.

The dried flowers already in the vase had looked dusty and jaded and she threw them away. They had been useful but now that the bright sunshine showed up dust and pointed accusingly at anything faded, they looked tawdry and spent.

'Oh for a host of golden daffodils,' she said.

'That I can manage!'

'Paul! Where did you get them?'

'A gift from a grateful patient, I believe.'

'Who?'

'I'm not sure. There was no card with

them and they arrived by messenger. Eileen took them in and he said they were for the lady of the house. That's you, so enjoy them and thank whoever it was who thought of you among your many admirers.'

Emma buried her nose in the earthy fresh scent and touched a stiff petal gently. 'Very fresh and a wonderful hint of spring.'

'Hadn't you noticed? Spring sprung a while ago and we missed it as we have been so busy. These are quite late daffodils. The orientals say that January and February and even March are the months of suicide and I believe them. Thank God we haven't had that among any of my patients but there's been a lot of depression.' He pointed to the brilliant sunlight. 'In my opinion that is the best medicine, so I think we should take time off and walk in the park for an hour.'

She arranged the flowers, using some to brighten the consulting room as well as their own drawing room and was ready to join Paul for their walk. The air was less warm than suggested by the sun and she found that she still needed a winter coat.

Paul held her hand as they walked across the park to say hello to the statue of Peter

Pan, and Emma drew him closer and put their linked hands in the pocket of her coat to keep warm. 'I should have worn gloves but I thought that I wouldn't need them again until the autumn.'

'How would you know? You haven't been for a walk for days and you work too hard. You need more fresh air.'

'Bea said that they had very bad weather again and the twins have colds. Who needs babies with runny noses?' she asked lightly.

'We do, but I'm glad that you seem happy. Are you happy, Emma?'

'Almost completely. I seldom think about it now and I'm really looking forward to Eileen having her baby. We have such a good life Paul, and I wouldn't change it for anything.' She looked up into his face. 'I mean it. No experience is wasted. I thought of that when I had the card from the manor house. I learned a lot from living there and I know it's possible to love and be loved by many people in various ways apart from my love for you.'

'Do you love many people?'

'I suppose not, unless I count ex-patients who formed a bond when they were very illl. That is a kind of love. The same goes for old colleagues who went through the war with me. I don't think about them often but when I meet them again I feel a rush of affection. I do love my aunts and Bea is special, and I still have a sneaking affection for people like Phillip and George but there are not many more.' She sighed. 'I wish I'd been closer to my parents but that was impossible and in many ways, although she tried to sound neglected, my mother was glad to see the back of me.'

'I love you. I'm completely tunnel-visioned about that,' Paul insisted.

'Not a single patient?' she teased. 'Not even one of the doting females who come to have far more sessions with you than is necessary?'

'Not even Mrs Molton, but I do have many good friends whom I value.'

'You have no relatives left so I can't form bonds there. Have you no aunts or cousins tucked away? Not even a horrid sister like Mick's sister Myra?'

'Not a soul. You'll have to make sure I never feel like a neglected orphan child,' he said solemnly, and laughed.

'You always seem so ... complete, Paul.'

'I've had to be, as I have spent a lot of time alone and to be honest, I enjoy my own company if I have to be alone, but now, I am only really complete when you are with me, and the aunts fill me with wonder at times!'

A sense of warm belonging made them smile and their silence was contented. They laughed at Peter Pan who had collected a halo of sparrows and a few extra pigeon droppings, splashes of white on the tiny carved animals that clustered round the statue. 'I'll bring the camera next time I come here. Bea will be very put out to see her favourite eternal boy covered in pigeon poo!'

'I wrote to Dwight's godfather,' Paul said.

'You think there is a danger of Dwight being called up to the reserve? The thought of that makes me cold all over.'

'He telephoned and was very concerned about the whole situation as there are signs that the Americans are moving towards a serious confrontation in Korea. The Nazis have been beaten and now the communists seem to be the main concern of the White House and the military, but he wasn't worried about Dwight. He seems to have squared the medical board there.'

'Can't they cast their minds back to the

war when Russia was our staunch ally? Remember Stalingrad and the wonderful, awful sacrifices the Russians made then?'

'Politics and military power ignore what they want to forget and people like MacArthur are power crazy.'

'You sound bitter. That's not like you.'

'It's easy to unroll maps and send men to war. We have to pick up the shreds and try to piece broken bodies and minds together while the powers-that-be just add up the numbers of casualties and say how brave they've been.'

'Did you disapprove of the last war?'

'I hated it as did every sane person, but it had to be fought. In that war we were fighting for our own land and our own survival and if we'd lost we'd have been in abject slavery, but this is not our affair and I can't see how either side will have a real victory; just a sordid fight that ends nowhere and solves nothing, and the danger of MacArthur attacking China across the Korean border makes my blood run cold.'

'Surely he wouldn't dare? We haven't fully recovered from the war and we couldn't fight China. We need time to recoup our losses and gain strength. Who would have thought that rationing could be here so long after the naval convoys had no need to guard the merchant ships? They can now sail alone in safety apart from odd mines floating about the ocean, but many things are still in very short supply.'

'We spent too much on the war and we certainly can't afford another. Even America, who seems like the land of plenty, is feeling the pinch. They can hardly afford the money spent on the Marshall Plan for Europe but they have to make sure that people can rebuild and grow crops and make things in the factories again or the situation would lead to anarchy.'

They walked back to the house and Eileen gave Paul a note. 'This fell out of the flowers and I found it in the hall,' she said.

He looked up from the note. 'Do you recall a time when I went out on house calls to a farm?'

'I remember that,' Eileen said. 'You brought back eggs each time you went there and I was sorry when it stopped.'

'Look on the bright side. It did mean I had no need to go there again as he was cured,' Paul replied mildly.

'The lad with agoraphobia?' Emma looked interested. 'He sent the flowers?'

Paul raised his eyebrows. 'He even brought them into London himself, but he was too shy to ask to see me. He must be feeling a lot more confident to travel into a big city.'

'And grateful.' Emma bent to smell the earthy scent of the daffodils. 'Why flowers? He came from an arable farm, didn't he?'

'I talked to his father and suggested that as an interim course he would be better working in an enclosed situation like a greenhouse, but he needed to work and not be treated as an invalid.'

'If he was afraid of open spaces he must have been terrified of large empty fields that he had to venture into for sowing and ploughing. Poor boy!'

'His father had a barn adapted with added high windows and he built another greenhouse close to the farmhouse so that Jeff had no need to walk in the open.'

'So he grows plants and flowers indoors?'

'He says that he loves the work and even now, after treatment, when he can walk in the fields again, he prefers to grow flowers and early vegetables.'

'How did he get like that?' Eileen wanted to know.

'A childish trick, when another older boy said he'd take him home by a short cut, pushed him into a field and took his bicycle and he had to walk home across rough ground without even his cycle lamp to show him the way in pitch darkness. He got hopelessly lost and panicked. He was only ten. After that he refused to leave the house alone and it got worse.'

'Until you cured him.'

Paul shrugged. 'He wanted to be cured and under hypnosis we sorted it out between us. It helps if the patient really wants to get better.'

'I wish you were my doctor for the baby,' Eileen remarked enviously.

Paul gave an exaggerated shudder. 'I do believe I'd faint. It was never my ambition to deliver babies, and if Emma was ill I'd call in the local GP.'

'Go on with you! You never would be scared of babies.' She went off to tell Mick about the flowers and to cook the carrots that were now her favourite food. Her body had thickened and she had the bloom of a healthy woman, content in her pregnancy, and Emma was genuinely happy for her.

'She looks well,' Paul remarked.

'The clinic is pleased with her and as she is safely over the first three months they said she can mix with more people and not worry about German measles, so poor Mick will have to take her to the cinema three times this week to catch up on her films.'

'You haven't been to a film for ages. You should get out more. Why not take her to one that I wouldn't enjoy!'

'And mop up her tears? I think that *Dangerous Moonlight* is on *again!* Anton Walbrook has a lot to answer for, driving impressionable girls mad with that sultry voice and those dark glasses! It's a wonder the film hasn't worn out.'

Eileen decided on *Now Voyager,* and Paul solemnly handed her a very large clean handkerchief and a bag of mint humbugs before Emma took her to the local cinema.

'This is nice.' Eileen sat back in the shabby velvet seat and shifted her body comfortably. The usherette flashed her torch along the row and Emma was pleased to see that all the other seats in the row were filled and there would be no need to get up for late comers.

The Pathé news was about to begin, with the familiar cockerel crowing at the audience. A French politician smiled frostily at President Truman behind a desk and they shook hands with no evident warmth or sincerity. A few shots of tanks and anti-aircraft guns being loaded onto a naval ship, and a shot of American soldiers boarding a transport aircraft, made Emma uneasy, although the bland voice of the reporter tried to make it sound as if the peacekeeping force planned for Korea would be just that, with no violence, no loss of life and just a lot of men enjoying each other's company.

The huge curtains came together and swished apart again to show the lowering of the safety curtain, then floated back again to soft piped music, with pastel spotlights making the fabric change from white to blue and gold and a lovely sunset pink. 'I want a dress that colour,' Eileen breathed, and sighed as an even prettier turquoise swept over the curtains. 'Or that one,' she added. 'I think it's lovely here. I always like this bit.'

Emma smiled. Maybe a coloured light or so at home would be enough to send

Eileen into ecstasies without the need for a film!

The trailers announcing coming attractions showed a bright American musical with the girls all farm fresh and small waisted with tight curls and conical breasts and a man in a white shirt open to the waist, singing that the corn was as high as an elephant's eye. Another film trailer was about the war, and the mud and anguish made a telling contrast to the musical. They were both 'U' films and could be seen by any age group.

*The Cruel Sea,* with the aristocratic face of Jack Hawkins, men with taut faces and lots of dark ships on leaden water looked exciting, and even Mick or Paul would want to see it.

The smell of mint humbugs fought the pungent odour of eucalyptus from a man with a graveyard cough in the row behind them and Emma hoped that the humbugs would win, but she turned up her coat collar when he coughed and blew his nose. She glanced at Eileen and wondered if her freely flowing tears would act as a personal antiseptic as she held the large damp handkerchief to her face, ready for the next emotional heart-tugging.

A Mickey Mouse cartoon and a dull account of keeping hens to add to the nation's diet, completed the programme and Eileen dried her eyes and sighed as they walked home. 'I feel better for a good cry. It was so sad,' she added happily.

Emma was restless and as Paul was out at a meeting and would be back late, she made a cake and some shortcakes, adding semolina and almond essence to lift the flavour to taste better and to vary the texture of the heaviness of dark flour. Once or twice she looked at the telephone but decided that if she phoned Aunt Emily at that time of night, she would think there was a crisis and be upset, although Emma knew that her aunt would be drinking tea as usual at that hour and have no plans for bed until midnight.

Paul came back very late. 'That's the worst of being given a lift. I had to stay until Ralph finished talking to an old friend and it was difficult to get away.'

'You look tired, and I am too.'

'Worn out by romantic films and Eileen rabbiting on about film stars?'

She frowned. 'Not really. Just restless, as if something is about to happen.'

'Don't get too much like Emily! It

can't be anything bad. Eileen isn't due yet and we have no psychopaths watching the house as far as I know! Is there enough milk for a decent cup of Horlicks?'

'Yes, I had the same idea. I'll heat the milk and we'll get to bed. I'll feel less tired tomorrow and the black dog will have gone.'

'You, with a black dog? He raised her face to his and kissed her gently. 'You are seldom depressed, so why now?'

'Nothing. I just feel restless and overtired and I had an urge to ring Aunt Emily, but I didn't.'

'Drink up and come to bed. We both need a good night. Tomorrow I have three patients but only one the day after that in the morning, so we'll go to Kew or somewhere to see a few flowers.'

She dreamed of the bluebell wood behind Mottistone Manor on the Island and heard a voice say, 'Don't pick them. They droop quickly and never look right in a vase, so leave them alone.'

'Do you think the bluebells at Kew are over?' she asked Paul at breakfast before they left.

'We'll see. I saw them once and stayed there for a long time just looking,' he admitted. 'It was early in the war before they turned a lot of the gardens over to growing vegetables and the railings were still there before they were taken to build Spitfires.'

'I went there too. How strange if we'd been there on the same day and not known each other.'

'The sun was shining and the blue of the flowers was reflected in the smooth copper-coloured tree bark of the wood.'

'I saw that and thought it wonderful. Let's go as soon as you finish with your patient.'

'It may have changed,' he warned cautiously.

'We'll risk it. Do we have enough petrol?'

'Plenty, as I walk a lot in London and you hardly ever use the car.'

Emma pulled on a velvet hat and scarf and put a thick rug in the car, although she doubted if the sun would be warm enough to let them sit out of doors, and by the time they reached Kew Gardens she felt her nagging depression lift. They walked by the river and ate bread and cheese and cider in the pub by the water then went into the gardens.

Emma shivered. 'It's colder than I thought.' They walked briskly to the wood but found only sagging leaves where the bluebells had finished for the year.

'Still cold?' Paul looked anxious and took her into the tropical plant house where the warm, steamy air hung heavily over the exotic plants.

'Warmer, but it's stifling in here. I want to go home Paul.'

He wrapped her in the rug and sat her in the back seat. 'You've been doing too much. A day in bed will put you right.'

She drowsed and was half asleep when they stopped at the house.

'Oh, there you are,' Mrs Coster called accusingly from the hallway. 'About time too.'

'What's wrong?'

Paul helped Emma up the steps and Mrs Coster stared. 'Blimey, two of them!'

'What do you mean?'

'Eileen looks just like you do, Sister. She's got the flu if you ask me.'

'Oh, no!' Emma slumped visibly and Mrs Coster took her by the arm and marched her up to bed, braving the lift that she really didn't trust and then helping Emma undress and get into bed.

Paul arrived with two hot water bottles and Emma lay shivering in the warm bed. She drank the aspirin mixture with a shudder and slept.

Paul went down to see Eileen. 'Right turn up for the books,' Mick said cheerfully. 'She's asleep and warm so what else can we do, Doc? They must have picked it up the other evening in the pictures. Eileen said there was this man with a cough behind them and there's a lot of it about.'

'Proper epidemic,' Mrs Coster said. 'Down in Peabody buildings they've all got it and the market lads are going down like flies.'

'I think you'd better not come in for a while, Mrs Coster. You have a large family to look after and can't afford to catch it.'

'Me, catch the flu? Not on your life! You'll want me here. Some of them are old enough to see to things and it's time my Maisie pulled her finger out and did something. These two aren't getting up for a week at least and they'll feel like wet rags so who will do the work and the cooking?

Mind you,' she added with an important expression, 'the hall will have to go if I am up here.'

'Thank you, Mrs Coster. The hall can go to hell,' Paul said fervently. 'You are a gem.'

'Well fancy that!' She tucked the bedclothes securely round Eileen's shoulders. 'They don't need a lot except drinks, so that isn't much trouble. By the way, Sister's aunt rang and wants you to ring back. Said it was important and not just a chat. Never rains but it pours,' she added and went upstairs to the kitchen, singing happily.

Paul dialled the number and was ready to wait for Emily Darwen to answer, but she must have been sitting by the phone because her voice came over the line almost at once. 'Is Emma there?'

'Not just now.'

'Good. Shut the door and I want to talk to you.'

He heard the tremor in her voice. 'What's wrong?' he asked.

'It's my sister Clare, Emma's mother.' Emily took a deep breath to help her compose herself. 'We've not been close, but it's a shock. She went in a coach to the Cotswolds and there was a bad accident. Three dead and five injured.'

'How bad is Mrs Dewar?'

'They rushed them to Southmead Hospital but she died a few hours later. Her doctor works in the district where most of the injured live, as they all go to the same chapel, and he heard about her and rang me. We had an arrangement that he would contact me if ever Clare was ill and needed help.' Her voice tailed off in a sob. 'Not much I could do, then or now. You'll tell Emma?'

'I'll tell her tomorrow. She has the flu and is asleep now.'

'Emma's ill? Someone must go to Bristol and sort things out there.'

'Not you. I'll see to everything. Go to Dr Sutton for a sleeping pill for tonight and I'll ring you when I hear anything more.'

'I'll give you the address and number of Clare's solicitor and the funeral is on Friday. Do you think I'm wicked not to go? I couldn't bear it, Paul.'

'Don't even think about it.'

Her tone lightened. 'I'll put the kettle on. Emma does know how lucky she is with you but I'd like to say so, too.'

'Praise indeed.' Paul spoke softly, moved by the few words from a woman who gave no false praise. 'And Emily ... we'll come down soon. Emma will need you yet again.'

'I'll be here.'

He stared at the silent phone, then gave a reluctant grin. 'So, I'll see to everything! A funeral in Bristol, two women with the flu and a busy practice to run!'

## Chapter Eight

The day had seemed endless but it was still fairly early as they had come back from Kew in a hurry and there was time for Paul to ring through to the solicitor's office in Bristol. He asked to speak to Mr Springer.

'Springer here.'

'I'm telephoning on behalf of my wife,' Paul began and told the lawyer the gist of what had happened so far as he knew the details. 'My wife has a bad attack of flu and will be unable to come to the funeral,' he added firmly when the lawyer wanted to speak to her personally.

'There are very few matters to consider,' Mr Springer said. 'Not many, as your wife's father made a will that covered this contingency.'

'Do you mean that Mrs Dewar has no will?'

'Ethics forbid me to disclose details over the telephone, Doctor, but there is no will written by her that would be valid, as he willed the house and contents to his wife for her lifetime and then to go to his daughter, but there are forms to sign and authorisation for the funeral expenses, and so on.' He coughed discreetly. 'And my fees, of course.'

'If I send a representative, can he or she deal with it by proxy?'

'Certainly, if the person brings a signed form from Mrs Sykes handing over complete power of attorney in this matter, but I must see someone here in my office after the funeral, before anything can be taken from the house. Of course, the house will be available for whoever you send, to use as a base until after the funeral and the will is read.'

'I know that my wife has a key.'

'As this unfortunate accident happened

so quickly and Mrs Dewar expected to return home after her outing, all the necessary services will be connected—water, gas and electricity and even the telephone—so if Mrs Sykes or another relative was to go there at this time, it would be like going home,' he added warmly. 'Not a happy homecoming, but familiar things count for something, and she would have the right to use the house.'

'We could find accommodation somewhere near, if you know of a hotel or a guest house?'

'Use the house. It's wise to have someone there to look after the property after a death. You've no idea how many times we've had to send people to court for stealing items from an unattended house. A cleaner might have a key or workmen doing jobs around the place are often tempted as they think that nothing will be missed by relatives who live far away and come just for the funeral, and a lot of animosity can occur when relatives accuse each other of taking something a little too soon! ... Stealing a march on the others, may we say? It has been known.'

'You've been most helpful, Mr Springer.

I know that my wife will be very relieved to hear that I have contacted you.'

Paul sat for a while in silence. A homecoming? He almost blessed the fact that Emma couldn't travel to Bristol. He imagined her alone in the house that she hated, with memories of tension and cold unhappiness between her mother and father and the lack of love given to their only daughter.

'Sorry Doc, I thought the office was empty. Just wanted to check the diary.' Mick riffled through the pages and gave a low whistle. 'Some weeks we are slack and now when Sister is under the weather, your diary is full, so you won't be going anywhere, will you?' His sharp eyes twinkled. 'Seems you need me to sort things out up there.'

'You?'

'Why not? Eileen isn't half as bad as Sister and she'll be up tomorrow, pottering about and doing for herself down in our flat, and Mrs Coster will answer the door and bully Sister and make her stay in bed, which leaves you to do what you're here for.'

'I was going to ring an old colleague in Bristol.' Paul looked at him seriously but with a touch of humorous respect. 'Why do I feel I'm being manipulated?'

'Because you are. People can't think straight if they are too close and from what I hear, both you and Sister will be better off away from that house.'

'You don't miss much!' Paul remarked dryly.

'Not a lot,' Mick agreed. 'Well, do I pack a bag and get up there for the funeral and see who else is there and report back to Madam?'

'Someone has to see the lawyer.' Paul sounded doubtful.

'I can do that, if that's what's worrying you. I'm quite good at interviews and legal matters. Did enough to save the boys from getting ripped off in hospital when they couldn't understand forms.'

'Probably better than I could,' Paul admitted.

'More than likely,' Mick asserted with satisfaction. 'Where do I kip?'

'In the house.' Mick raised his eyebrows and Paul repeated the gist of what he'd heard from Mr Springer.

'It makes sense, and if I have a key I can come and go as I please and make sure it's all locked up when I'm not there. Can you ask Sister who would be likely to have keys, not that it seems as if Mrs Dewar would leave keys with just any old neighbour!'

'The only one that Emma mentioned was a woman who made a lot of mischief between her parents and seemed to have a hold over Mrs Dewar. They went everywhere together and it was she who organised the trips from the chapel.'

'That's the old biddy I'll have to watch.' Mick sounded ebullient. 'Sounds interesting. I know what happens. Myra did what you said the lawyer told you. She went into my Gran's house and took away a load of stuff before the rest of us could see the rabbit!'

'Don't expect to be a suspicious private eye. Surely one respectable chapel-going old lady wouldn't be like that?'

'Often the worst,' Mick replied cynically. 'Specially if they are the same size.'

'What can you mean? Not her clothes? Who would want a dead woman's clothes?'

'You'd be surprised.'

'I learn something not in any textbooks every day with you around.' Paul laughed weakly. 'Here is the train timetable. Look up a train and at least I can drive you to the station. I'll make out a power of attorney and ask Emma to sign it.'

'I can be ready in fifteen minutes.'

'You'll go tonight? What's the hurry?'

'I know where I'm needed and it isn't here. I'll just manage to catch the next train from Paddington if we hurry and I'll get something to eat on the way as that train has a buffet.'

'Which reminds me. You'll have expenses. Be sure you use a taxi in Bristol, from the station, to the funeral and when you go to see the solicitor as his offices are down in the city and may not be on a bus route. Take it,' Paul insisted when Mick drew away from the money as if he wanted to refuse it. 'There may be other things you have to pay for and I don't want you to stint yourself. You are doing us a big favour.'

'Makes a change. Boot's usually on the other foot. See you downstairs, Doc. I'll pack and get the car out.'

Emma signed the letter languidly, only too thankful to make no real decisions and Eileen was frankly envious of Mick's adventure but admitted that she felt like a wrung-out floor cloth and would use the time until she felt stronger to make more baby clothes.

'The baby has more energy than I have,' she grumbled, as she felt lively kicking.

'Try to enjoy yourself and see something of Bristol if you get the chance. It's a good city. Don't hurry back and Mick ... thank you,' Paul said when he left Mick at Paddington Station.

'My pleasure. I'm not hung up over this as I never met Sister's mother and you know me, always like putting my nose where it isn't wanted.'

He hurried to the platform and was settling in his seat when the whistle blew and the train started off for the West Country and after Bristol, Wales. Someday, we'll take the baby to Wales, he promised himself. Never been there but I like hills and mountains. You can keep the sea.

It seemed odd to have a compartment almost to himself. His memories of transport by train were very different: men crowded into every possible seat and every foot of corridor and the smell of damp kitbags and Wills Woodbine cigarettes, sweat and often unwashed bodies if the troops were on their way back from abroad. I'll miss the next lot. In a way it had been good with the lads and a damn good CO but there were other things now, Eileen and the baby, the Doc and his missus and security, something he'd defend to the last if necessary but in Kensington if possible, and not in some benighted battlefield.

His fifty-shilling suit, off-the-peg from a famous retailer, fitted well and he looked down at the colour, a nice dark green with a shirt of light brown. Eileen had wanted him to have the ox-blood material but it was a bit over the top for his taste. The green went well with his regimental tie and the new trilby hat was rakish but good-looking. In his case was a dark grey raincoat which would cover the suit for the funeral. Chapel service, so they'd be dressed in black or grey. Hope it isn't a hot day, he thought glumly. The coat was warm.

Lights from villages and small towns made the twilight alive, and on the roads that crossed the railways and in the country lanes, there were no armoured cars and no tanks making the countryside sinister, but there were still signs of wartime bombing and whole streets were boarded up to await reconstruction in the towns.

Rogue bushes and swathes of creeper made the ruins softer and hid the scars and then at last, Bristol Temple Meads Station, the building designed by Isambard Kingdom Brunel, opened up to the incoming trains, it's façade triumphantly complete, overshadowing the rubble of war where the city was laid flat and the sad remnants of historic buildings often tottered and fell before they could be saved.

Mick waited for a taxi and eyed the station front with awe. More like a palace than a station, he thought and watched the hundreds of starlings sweep and wheel over the roofs before settling to roost there for the night. The twilight was golden and rose-streaked. The baby will be born before the days shorten, he thought. They said July and he hoped it would keep fine for the nappy-washing. His face relaxed into a fond smile. What a turn up! Him a father.

'This is the address. I don't know how far. It's my first visit,' he said to the driver of the cab. 'I want to book a car for a funeral. How do I do that?'

'My mate does that side of things. He'll fix you up and if you need it again just give him a ring. You'll leave from this address on the day?'

'Yes, the funeral is at two in the afternoon, so he'd best come early.' Mick told him which cemetery it would be and the driver nodded.

'Take him twenty minutes from the house to the church and then another fifteen to the cemetery and he'll wait to bring you back so you'll need him for half a day. Will you be following the hearse from that house?'

Mick stared in horror. 'You mean the woman's corpse might be with me all night?'

'If that's where she died.'

'It was a road accident and she died in hospital.'

'Well, chances are she's in their mortuary and will be taken from there.'

'Thank God for that! I never met the lady in life and I don't want to meet her afterwards!'

'Ex-service?' asked the driver who had noticed the tie and the sturdy set of Mick's shoulders.

'Very much so. Invalided out. You in that lot?'

'Gloucesters. They say we may go back and I'll not be sorry. It's a good mob and I've a lot of friends there. My wife was bombed and I might as well serve again, as a driver if I'm lucky.'

'It's a good regiment. Aren't they the ones who can wear two cap badges, front and rear, from a time when they fought back to back in some old shindig and won a lot of glory?'

'Yeah, that's the only thing that gets my craw! Marching through Gloucester on parade with bayonets fixed to show we have the freedom of the city. More spit and polish but not a penny extra,' he grumbled.

'It may never happen,' Mick said and paid the fare as the cab drew up in front of the only completely dark house in the road. 'Your mate will be here on time?'

'Needs the work, Mate. Don't we all.'

Mick looked up at the empty windows, then took the key Emma had given him and let himself into the hall. He put down his case and swore softly when he nearly tripped over a large heavy suitcase. He found a light switch and cautiously peeped into each room just to make sure no coffin was there. 'Phew! Even without a corpse this place is spooky. Must be the chilly evening.'

The day had been mild but by evening

had grown colder, and it was now nightfall. He went into the living room to look for heating and switched on the electric fire in a hearth that had never seen a piece of coal. In the kitchen he found tea and a half-full jug of milk that was rapidly turning to cheese. Well it wouldn't be the first time he'd had his tea black. There was a toaster and a whole loaf of bread, and in the cupboard sardines and Spam and a piece of cheese. Margarine and a pot of plum jam added to the store of discoveries and he knew he wouldn't starve overnight.

He took his case upstairs and found the main bedroom which was strangely untidy in the rather austere house. Clothes were lying on the bed and on the chairs and drawers were half open. In the other big room the bed was stripped and everything looked scrubbed and empty, but the bed in the small room was made up and the room tidy. He opened his case and took out pyjamas. A hot drink and toasted sandwich and bed, he decided. He recalled Emily Darwen saying that her sister liked to have a teacher lodging during the week in the winter term time so that she wouldn't be alone in the house on dark winter nights, and the occasional local preacher could spend a weekend in her small room if he was preaching at the chapel, which explained the made-up bed.

Mick decided to use this bed rather than make up the one in the other room, but he unpacked his own towel that Eileen had suggested he brought with him. 'You never know who has been using the ones they have in a strange place,' she said, as if he would catch some disease from the sterile, forbidding house.

The smell of toast made the kitchen more homely and he took his tray to the sitting room where the only electric fire was giving out welcome heat. In the relative comfort, he started when the front door bell rang. A man and woman stood by the door, a step back from the porch as if expecting something bad. 'Hello,' Mick said and grinned.

'We wondered, that is I saw a light and we ...' the woman said, hesitantly.

'I thought we ought to see if everything was all right,' the man added.

'Very nice of you.' Mick stood back. 'You'll be the neighbours, I reckon. Come in, I could do with a chat about things.'

'Who are you? We haven't seen you

before.' The woman eyed him with suspicion and her husband pushed her into the hall.

'He's all right, Judy, but we ought to know what you are doing here and how you got in.'

'That's easy. I had a key from Mrs Sykes, the daughter of Mrs Dewar. Unfortunately, Mrs Sykes is ill with the flu and so she sent me to sort out things here and go to the funeral.'

'Are you Mr Sykes?'

'Lord no! I'm their gofer, so to speak. I work for them and her husband is a doctor.'

'I never knew that, but I remember her when she used to be here. Very pretty and always a nice smile and a good morning, unlike her mother.'

'Never speak ill of the dead, Judy.'

'Why not?' Mick asked blandly. 'I take it that you were not on friendly terms, if you didn't know that the daughter was married to a very important doctor.'

The woman eyed the cup of black tea. 'Do you drink it like that?'

'No choice as the milk's gone off.'

'Wait a minute and I'll bring some milk. Not much of a welcome, sour milk! You'd think she would have left some if she knew you were coming for the funeral.'

'She couldn't do that if she's dead! It's only to be expected as the house was empty and shut up. Who could be expected to leave me anything?'

'My name's Arthur Smythe and this is Judy my wife. Go and get the milk Jude, and a bottle of beer. You eat up your sandwich before it goes rock hard, Mr ...'

'Grade. Mick Grade, Arthur and I'm very pleased to meet you.'

'So am I glad to meet you. When we saw her come in earlier we thought she had permission but Judy didn't like it. She knew that Mrs Dewar had a daughter who was away and Mrs Hammond was always in and out of the house, but now after the accident, we wondered if she had the right to be here as she's not family.'

Judy Smythe came back with the milk. She put a hand to the teapot and made a face. 'Can I make a fresh cup if we are staying?'

'Please stay. I think there are one or two matters to clear up here. I'll get two glasses,' he added when he saw Arthur open the bottle of beer. 'Tea's fine but that looks better.'

Judy laughed. 'Beer? Mrs Dewar would turn in her grave.' She clapped a hand over her mouth and looked uneasy.

'Don't worry, she can't hear you. Strict chapel wasn't she?' Mick relaxed and told them about Emma and Paul and Eileen. 'Now this woman who was here. Does she have a key? I wondered what was going on as there is a bit of a mess upstairs as if someone has been going through cupboards and drawers.'

'Didn't I say?' Judy was triumphant. 'Did she know you were coming here?'

'No, and we wouldn't have known about the accident but for Mrs Dewar's sister who was in touch with her doctor in case her sister needed help at any time. It's been awkward, as Mrs Dewar would have nothing to do with her relatives and yet they felt obliged to keep an eye on her in case of emergency. Her doctor rang her sister on the Isle of Wight and she told Mrs Sykes.'

'Are you going to the funeral?'

'That's why I'm here, and to see the solicitor the morning after the funeral.'

Arthur looked at his wife, a question

hovering between them. 'We thought of going as neighbours to show respect, but I don't know.'

'Why doesn't Arthur come with me? I have a car coming to collect me and you'd be doing me a favour if you can spare the time.'

'I'm retired now and I've time in plenty so I'd like that. I can point out different people who might have known her better than she knew us. She was always tight-lipped when she saw us as we used to speak to her daughter when she was here and she didn't like it. Very possessive, she was.'

'You can come back to tea,' Judy offered. 'I don't suppose her friend will give away much and there's nothing here.'

'Have you any shillings? Change for a ten shilling note? I see the gas is on meter and I want a bath tomorrow if that geyser doesn't blow up!'

Mick whistled to himself as he turned off the fire and went upstairs to bed. Thank God for nosy neighbours, he thought. They would look after the house if necessary, and he'd be glad of Arthur's company at the funeral.

The sun woke him as it shone through the thin curtains and he stretched and grinned. Not a bad night's sleep and the day might be interesting. Arthur had told him of a café about half a mile away used by men off the night shift at the aircraft factory and used also by local people to eke out their rations, so he didn't bother with breakfast but decided to explore the possibility of a fry-up that he hadn't cooked for himself.

He hesitated before leaving. It was unlikely that the woman would return before the funeral but to make sure that the house was safe, he bolted the front door and put on the safety chain and took the back door key that was in the lock and went out that way, locking the door behind him.

There were shops and a fish and chip shop near the café that might be useful if he needed an evening meal. He returned to the house to brush his shoes and tidy up, after a big breakfast that would last him until the evening and Judy's tea.

Arthur arrived early, obviously intrigued by the situation and dressed in grey with a black tie. 'I feel a fraud but Jude said I must put on this tie, so here I am! Everyone is going to wonder who you are, Mick. They'll think you are with me rather than the other way round. I can't wait to see the sour faces trying to guess.'

The harmonium was playing a hymn as they walked up the path to the chapel and a tall minister fell into step with the two men and eyed them curiously.

Mick smiled and held out his hand. 'I'm here to represent Mrs Sykes, the daughter of the deceased,' he said formally.

'I see.' It was obvious that he didn't see, and still seemed puzzled as they paused in the doorway to the chapel.

'Something wrong, Padre?'

'No, of course not. It's good to see you here,' he said hurriedly. 'It's just that I understood that Mrs Dewar had no near relatives and that her friend would organise everything.'

'That's odd. Mrs Sykes is her daughter, married to a leading doctor in London and there are several sisters who Mrs Dewar chose to ignore over the past few years, but they kept in touch with the doctor here to make sure they could be called on if Mrs Dewar ever needed help or nursing, even if she was a complete ... even if she wouldn't have anything to do with them.'

The poor man seemed even more confused. 'But Mrs Hammond was so positive when I asked about relatives.'

'Did you ask her doctor?'

'No, she said there was no need and she'd be in touch with the solicitor after the funeral.'

'Jumped the gun a bit, didn't she?'

'What do you mean?'

'Someone with a key has turned the place over,' Mick said bluntly. 'She has a key.'

'I'm sure you must be mistaken. I can't say more now as the hearse has arrived. I suppose if you are representing the daughter you must sit in the front pew,' he said unhappily. 'We must do everything in the correct manner.' They followed him into the building and he bent over a woman dressed entirely in black. She looked very annoyed but changed her seat and sat in the row behind, leaving the front seats for Mick and Arthur, and Mick felt that her baleful gaze bore into his back.

There were about a dozen mourners. The coffin had four wreaths on it, one from her sisters Emily Darwen and Janey, one from Emma, ordered by the solicitor, and one from the chapel congregation. The other was from Mrs Hammond and Mick was pleased to note that it was a poor affair and paled in beauty beside the one that the lawyer had chosen after Paul had made certain that a really good wreath would be sent.

That will make them talk, Mick thought with satisfaction and opened his hymn book.

## Chapter Nine

The field that did duty as an annexe to the original cemetery seemed a long way out. The old cemetery was conveniently close to the local church and chapel, but this was over a mile away from the houses of the old village and had nothing to show that it belonged to any particular sect. A far-sighted but unimaginative planner had prepared for the future as more houses were built and a huge housing estate was planned that would spill over, eventually almost to the gates of the new burial ground, engulfing old properties, and a small neglected park that was the dog walkers' main access to greenery, and a battered swing and slide, were all that remained of a children's playground.

As yet, there were few graves in the new cemetery, most of them covered with grassy mounds of turf that had contracted in the hot dry spell that left gaps between them as there was nobody to water the grass. No grave as yet had a headstone, and a modest wooden building with a cross over the porch was the only sign that this was an official cemetery with religious connections.

Mick looked at the wide empty field with distaste. It could have been a place where war graves contained many dead, buried without due ceremony.

He recalled Sunday afternoons when his mother took him to put flowers on his Gran's grave and they met a lot of people they knew while they cut stems and tidied the grass and weeded the marble chippings within the rectangular grave edgings. At that time he had been bored and used the afternoons chasing the other children in and out of the avenues made by Victorian tombstones and the white winged angels that towered over the last resting places of the more prosperous local shopkeepers and council officials. Usually he'd run too fast and slipped, grazing his knees on the gravel but the scabs were fascinating to pick off when he sat on the lavatory so he didn't really mind the slight inconvenience.

He discovered that he was shocked by this bleak and soulless place. 'Might as well bury her in the back garden,' he muttered, forgetting how he'd derided the old Sunday afternoons among the trees and statues. 'Who's likely to come out all this way to see to a grave?'

'Not many,' Arthur said. 'Most get cremated these days and have their names in a remembrance book, somewhere.'

The freshly-dug clay sat in huge clods by the open grave and the coffin was lowered onto the earth, covering another decaying coffin containing the body of Clare Dewar's husband.

'Together again in their last resting place,' the minister said, trying for a happy note among the tense group by the grave, and Mrs Hammond looked disapproving as if she hated imagining her friend in such close proximity to the man with whom marriage had been a disaster for both of them.

Mick Grade shook hands with the minister and handed him an envelope. 'A donation to the chapel from Mrs

Sykes, daughter of the deceased, Padre,' he explained and hurried Arthur away to the car before the other mourners could speak to him.

'Phew, I'm hot!' Mick shed the raincoat and hat and loosened his tie.

'Back to the house,' Arthur suggested. 'A nice cup of tea would be just the job.'

'I have to see the lawyer at nine tomorrow,' Mick said.

'I'll pick you up at eight-thirty.' The driver eyed Mick hopefully. 'Staying long? I'm cheaper by the day.'

'Let me pay you up to date now and we can discuss that tomorrow after I've seen the man. It depends on what I have to do, but I think I'll need you for at least another day.'

'You needn't have paid him now,' Arthur said.

'He earned it and I think he's skint. Not easy to get custom now the troops have gone. The Yanks paid anything and the officers out at the airfield must have used them a lot, too.'

'I thought you didn't know this part?'

'At our reunion I talked to a bloke who drives a cab he bought after his demob. He finds it hard and can't wait to get back in the army and go off to Korea. He said it's the same in any big city where they did well during the war. When the troops left army bases and in places like Portsmouth where the Navy thinned out a bit, shops felt the pinch and local people couldn't afford cabs. We used to say, "Don't you know there's a war on?" when supplies were short or you couldn't get anything done in your house, but a lot of people would like the war back, as they made a lot out of it.'

Judy was eager to hear about the funeral and as Mick described the mourners, she and Arthur nodded and gave names to them, Judy adding her own often caustic comments. 'I suppose Mrs Hammond was in black?'

'Like a crow waiting for a corpse,' Mick said cheerfully. 'Sorry, that wasn't nice.' He glanced at the clock.

'Not meeting anyone, are you? We hoped you'd have a bite to eat with us tonight.'

'I'll go back now and sort a few things and I think I may have a visitor who will not be pleased to see me, but later, I'd like to bring in fish and chips for us all for supper if that suits you. You've been very kind. Don't know how I could have stood it today without Arthur.'

'You think she'll come back?'

'Bound to, before the lawyer checks on the house, and seeing me here at the funeral; she'll wet herself when the padre tells her who I am and why I'm here.'

'I'll take my knitting and sit in the front window. I wouldn't miss this for the world,' Judy said.

'And I ought to water the front garden,' Arthur grinned. 'If you need any help just give a whistle.'

Mick changed from his suit into a short-sleeved shirt and light trousers and made tea. He unbolted the front door and slid back the safety chain so that anyone with a key could enter easily. He sat in the sunlit room and waited.

The newsagent had not been told to cancel the daily papers and by now there were a few copies on the mat so Mick read the local news and thought it was the same as any other parochial paper he'd read. He made a note to cancel the papers and the milk and then tried to do the crossword puzzle in the first copy and looked at the answers in the following day's issue. He read the advertisements for garden produce, and wished he could carry a sack of onions home with him as they were in short supply in London. He envied Arthur who had a long productive strip at the back of his house and it was full of vegetables.

Mick grinned. Arthur's front garden was saturated from the watering and he was now grubbing up grass from between the stones of the path. If she didn't appear soon and put them all out of their misery he would have the tidiest garden in the road.

A small car stopped at the gate and backed into the driveway, almost up to the front door. 'Wise woman,' Mick muttered. 'Heavy cases take a lot of heaving if she has to carry them far.'

He heard the key in the lock and stood back out of sight. Mrs Hammond came in carrying a suitcase that was obviously empty and hurried upstairs. She was still dressed in her full set of mourning clothes. Mick followed silently and stood in the doorway of the main bedroom while she folded clothes and packed them into the case. She half turned and saw him and gave a muted scream.

'Who are you and what are you doing here?'

'I might ask you the same, Madam.' Mick held up a winceyette nightdress. 'You missed one.'

'Get out before I call the police.'

Mick sat on the bedside chair. 'Carry on; the phone's in the hall. I want to speak to them too.'

'Who are you and why are you here spreading lies about me to our minister? How did you get into the house?'

'You saw me at the funeral and I assume the minister told you that I represent Mrs Sykes? I have a key and I have a right to be here, which is more than you have now that Mrs Dewar is dead.'

'I have every right! Mrs Dewar said that if she went before I did, I was to have any little thing I fancied and she'd put it in writing.' She sounded triumphant but wary. 'I came to see that the house was safe, and thought that I'd tidy up as she was killed so suddenly and there is a lot to do here.'

'*Clean up* more like,' Mick replied bluntly. 'One large suitcase packed in the hall and that one nearly full and who knows what in your handbag.' He picked up the canvas bag and began to undo the straps.

178

'Leave that alone!'

Mick backed away, still opening the large canvas holdall that was heavy and sounded metallic when he moved it. 'I think the police would call this burglars' swag,' he said calmly. 'Nice bit of silver she has, or had, if I wasn't here.'

'I thought I'd keep it safe,' she retorted desperately.

'And send it to the daughter that the minister had no idea existed? Pull the other one, it has bells on it!'

'She said I could help myself, and she knew I admired that teapot and jug.'

'And all the rest? You have that in writing?'

'She said the solicitor has it.'

'But you've never seen it? Sorry, Mrs Hammond; it's only your word if there's no proof, but I shall see the lawyer tomorrow and find out what's what, and even if she's left permission, you can't touch it until after the lawyer says you can.'

'You'll be gone tomorrow.' Her face relaxed. 'The lawyer will want someone to sort out her things and I'll tell him what a friend I've been all these years when her own daughter did nothing for her,' she added viciously.

'Dry old sticks, lawyers. He'll deal with facts, not sentiment, but give me your address and I'll be in touch, if she's left you anything.' He held out his hand but she ignored it and looked superior as if she thought she was getting the upper hand.

'Don't try to get round me. I don't want to shake your hand!'

'I don't, either. I want the key to this house. Until you hear otherwise, you have no right here, so hand it over and let me get on with sorting things out. I won't ask you to put it all back,' he added with mock kindness. 'I'll see to it.'

She looked furious but rummaged in her purse and handed him the key. She looked round the room and picked up a fur jacket from the bed, saw the cynical twist to his mouth and put it back. 'She promised it to me,' was her last effort at defiance, then almost ran down the stairs and slammed the front door after her.

Arthur turned off the hose and wound it on the drum. 'Careful, the path's a bit wet. You sent her off with a flea in her ear!'

Mick looked grim. 'If I hadn't come early, she'd have stripped the place. I could do with a sharp walk to get her off my mind, so even if it's a bit early,

I'll get the fish and chips now if you don't mind eating soon? After supper I'll phone the doc and tell him what happened.'

It was good to be with friendly undemanding people and as he walked briskly to the chip shop, Mick was able to see the funny side of his encounter, recounted later to the Smythes. Judy was fascinated and he knew that by the next meeting, Mrs Hammond would have lost her reputation among the ladies of the local Women's Institute.

'More tea?' Judy asked. Mick patted his stomach and smiled. 'Nothing, more. I feel fine. They do a good crisp batter in that chippy but I'd better phone now. The doc will want to know and I think I'll make a rough inventory of the house contents just to be on the safe side.'

'Anything really valuable?'

Mick shrugged. 'I haven't looked in the cupboards but Mrs H had a collection of silver in her bag, which she kindly returned.'

'Can she get in again?'

'Not unless she had two keys and from the look she gave me, that was the only one. I'd like you to keep it until we have this settled. Sorry to bother you but when

181

I go back there may be people wanting to view the house as I think it might be put up for sale.'

'It will give me something to do,' Arthur said. 'I'll act as caretaker and let you know what happens.'

'My bet is that Mrs Sykes will want to be rid of everything here. It wasn't a happy place for her although she did her best to be friendly with her parents. If she says what I think she'll say, the house and contents will go for auction. Best to be out of it quickly.'

Arthur looked thoughtful. 'You seem sure that the will is in her favour? You'll have egg on your face if she's given it all to Mrs Hammond or a cats' home.'

Mick smiled grimly. 'That old bag doesn't know yet but Mr Dewar willed the house and contents to his wife for her lifetime and then to his daughter, so she had no say in the matter.'

'How do you know that?'

'My boss spoke to the lawyer over the phone and he said as much. No details, as she wasn't buried but enough to show how the wind blows.'

Judy laughed. 'If there's a sale in the house, I'll be there and so will half the

182

neighbourhood. Imagine Mrs Hammond having to pay for anything she wants!'

With a good meal and a glass of beer, tea and bread and butter inside him, Mick went back to the unwelcoming house. He telephoned London and to his delight Eileen answered the phone. 'What are you doing, up at this hour, love?' he asked severely. 'You're supposed to have the flu!'

'I'm much better now and I said I'd do my sewing in the office until bedtime so that the doc could have supper with Sister. She's on the mend, but she was much more poorly than I was. What's happening up there?'

'I'll tell you about it later but I ought to speak to himself.'

'Hang on, I'll get him on the house phone.'

A minute later, Paul took up the phone and Mick gave him a lurid and concise account of his visit to Bristol. 'I'll see the lawyer tomorrow early and let you know what he says, later on in the day.'

'You're doing a grand job, Mick. The thought of Emma having to face all that makes me shudder.'

'What do you want done with the house and her things?'

'Emma wants everything sold and hopes that you can cope with the arrangements, but we do need you back here as soon as possible.'

'I got friendly with the neighbours. I think that Sister will remember them. He's ex-service like me and retired now. I'd trust him to caretake until the sale.'

'Ask the solicitor what the going rate for that is as they use caretakers a lot in these cases, and it's good to know of one we'd trust. Make make sure you pay him a fair price, Mick.'

'Anything else Doc?'

Paul hesitated. 'Emma says get rid of everything, but when you go through the contents, look for anything that might have a connection with Emma's grandmother or aunts and bring them here. I'll sort them out and Emma can choose what she wants to keep.'

'How will I know which to bring?'

'Difficult, but I feel that some of Emma's childhood is there and there may be something that she'd value.'

'Who would know?'

'Emma's Aunt Emily!' Paul gave a sigh of relief. 'You've spoken to her on the phone and she'll want to know what's happening, so after you see the solicitor and have permission to sort out the effects, make a list of anything that might be interesting and phone Miss Darwen. She'll tell you what to keep. Remember, you have complete power of attorney, Mick, and my deepest thanks. Feel free to give away anything to your new friends there before the sale.'

'I was thinking ...'

'Good,' Paul replied dryly.

'The friend I told you about is a terrible old woman but she *was* her friend. I gave her a hard time and she deserves something.'

Paul chuckled. 'I'd love to see you being Lord Bountiful but I'll leave that to you! It's a good idea and I know that Emma will approve.'

'Sure that Sister will want nothing much? There's a nice fur jacket?'

'Certainly not that! She'd hate to be reminded of her mother wearing it.'

'Right. I'll get it all under way and be home in a couple of days. Can I speak to Eileen again?'

'What is there left to do? I miss you, Mick.'

'That goes for me too, and I'll be home

as soon as possible.' He was relieved to hear her voice, now much stronger, and managed to make her laugh about his visit to Bristol.

'Sounds like a nice house.' She sounded wistful. 'And being sold off as if it doesn't matter any more seems really sad.'

'You'd hate it, Love. I wouldn't change it for our nice flat, not if they paid me! I can't see anyone having a baby here and my son will want a house where he can laugh and have some good times.'

'Your daughter, you mean,' Eileen said sharply.

'You've asked it what it is? I know it kicks. Nearly had me out of bed a couple of times,' he teased her. 'I didn't know it could talk.'

'I heard that if the man is quick off the mark after the curse is over, the baby is a girl, and you are always a bit ready and waiting for your oats!'

'I could do with some now.' His voice was low and urgent and explicit.

'Mick! Not over the phone! The girls in the exchange will hear!'

'Why not brighten their evening?'

'You are terrible,' she said tenderly. 'Come home soon.'

Mick was far too alert to feel sleepy and there was work to be done, so he took his notebook and pencil and began to list the contents of the kitchen cupboards and then the furniture in the main rooms. He left all the packaged foods and other edibles on the kitchen table for Judy to take and use and lifted the heavy suitcases onto the spare bed before he emptied out the clothes that Mrs Hammond had packed.

He grinned. Obviously Mrs Dewar had an obsession with warm winceyette nightdresses and knitted bed socks as there were enough to last her for years of frosty nights.

He packed one case with clothes and underwear, and wrapped shoes in news-paper in another case with toilet articles and hair brushes. He was glad to see the last of the personal things and thought that shoes carried the imprint of the dead woman and they gave him the creeps.

One medium-sized suitcase had a torn label on it with Emma Dewar written in large letters, so he put it aside, knowing that it must have belonged to Emma Sykes before she was married, when she was a nurse in training. Inside were her nursing diplomas and a few photographs of friends in uniform and some letters, duplicated in miniature to save weight and space as were letters from forces abroad during wartime when sent by air. There was even a certificate to state that Emma Dewar, aged nine, had passed the test for swimming at the local baths. He put them back carefully and looked for other intimate souvenirs.

In the roll-top desk was a bundle of letters addressed to Clare Dewar from a soldier during the First World War. Mick was suddenly sad and felt as if he was intruding. So she had been in love once, even if it wasn't with her husband, or at least a man had loved her and she had kept his letters, either for sentiment or a sense of power? He hesitated before adding them to the case, thinking that Emily Darwen might like them even if Emma didn't want to see them.

A folder of sepia-coloured prints of men and women dressed in Victorian and Edwardian clothes looked interesting and Mick added them to the case, hoping he'd remember to mention them to Miss Darwen when he rang her.

Under a piece of newspaper at least twenty years old there was a portrait of a woman with severely arranged dark hair and fine dark eyes. She had a lovely, but sad face. A cameo brooch at her throat among the lace of her high collar was her only adornment but the whole picture was far too arresting to be hidden in the bottom of a drawer for so many years.

Carefully he put it in the case with the items he had sorted out to take away, making sure it was flat and protected. That'll be her gran, he decided.

Mick yawned. Tomorrow would do for the rest after he'd seen the lawyer. He put the list of queries on the dining room table, made sure he had his identity card and his power of attorney in his wallet and everything ready for an early start in the morning, and then went to bed.

## Chapter Ten

'Who did you say?'

'Mick Grade. You must remember me, Miss Darwen. I answer the phone quite often when you ring your niece in London.'

Emily still sounded uneasy. 'Why doesn't she ring me? Is something wrong? Where is the doctor?'

'Nothing is wrong. I'm phoning from Bristol from your sister's house. Dr Sykes asked me to come here and sort out a few matters and attend the funeral, as neither he nor Sister could come here. Mrs Sykes had the flu quite badly but is getting better now and the doc had a lot of work that couldn't be put off so they sent me.'

'Of course!' Emily laughed with relief. 'Your wife is having a baby! I just didn't recognise your voice for a moment, and I hate the phone. Nasty, unfriendly things. I like to see who I'm talking to.'

'I was asked to ring you to see what I should keep from the house here. The lawyer says to go ahead with disposing of everything if that's what they want, but the doc suggested that you might have some idea of what Sister might like to have, or if there is anything that belonged to your family that you and your sister might want to keep.'

Emily sniffed. 'Not much from that house. I know I shouldn't speak ill of my own sister, especially now she's dead but she was a cold, hard woman and Emma was better out of it. Mean too, except for her own needs. Clare always liked clothes. She spent as little as possible on making a comfortable home and cooking decent meals but she hated having less than anyone in the family so she did spend something on appearances in the house to impress people, even copying our mother in making her house similar to hers as she had very little originality herself. She had crimson flock wallpaper because Mother had it and the same carpets as near as possible, but she kept a poor table. She lashed out on a fur coat and a jacket because none of us had one. The coat got the moth badly,' she added with satisfaction.

'That's the impression of her I get here.'

'I don't know why I'm telling you all this. I'd forgotten until I heard she died. How did you find things in Bristol? Did you feel embarrassed having to see to the will? That's if she left anything to Emma.'

'She had no choice as Mr Dewar had willed everything to his daughter after her mother's death. It was all tied up and even a woman who swore that Mrs Dewar had promised her a lot in writing, couldn't claim anything as the will was explicit and Mrs Dewar couldn't even have sold the house if she'd wanted to do so.'

'So at the last, Emma's father did the right thing and knew what she was like. I never gave him the credit for much but that showed a bit of sense,' she remarked, as if it cost her to approve of anything that Emma's father did.

'I made a list for you to check before I get rid of anything on it. The house is up for auction and there will be a house sale next week when the auctioneers will have labelled everything with lot numbers.' Mick spoke crisply before Emily could travel further down memory lane.

He mentioned the letters from the soldier and Emily said, 'Burn them. She sent him to the war when he was far too sensitive a man to bear the hardship and she never really wanted him until it was too late and then she made a terrible fuss.' Her voice broke. 'He was a nice boy. She and a friend of hers sent him a white feather because he hadn't volunteered for the army. It mattered a lot in those days to be called a coward in that way and there were posters everywhere telling young men that it was their duty to fight for King and Country. It was a silly thing for Clare and her friend to do to a man like him. It was before conscription so he had no need to go. He died and she married Sergeant Dewar on the rebound when she found her chances dwindling.'

'Right,' Mick said. 'Can do. I shall be having quite a bonfire before I leave, so I can add the letters to the piles of *Women's Weeklys* and other magazines she's hoarded for years.' He read out the long list and Emily said yes or no to all of the items.

'The portrait of my mother must go to Emma but I'd like to have it framed well first. I never knew that Clare had it as she told me it had been destroyed years ago. Keep the trinkets until I see them as some may be mine! I doubt if any of them are valuable. The silver was Janey's but she forgot it and didn't ask Clare for it and some of the ornaments sound like some I gave to my mother, so I'll have them back again. As for the rest, get rid of them and thank you for doing what must be a sad and onerous task.'

'My pleasure. I enjoyed doing battle with Mrs Hammond and now I shall be generous and give her a lot of clothes and kitchen things. It will be nice to see her torn between greed and her acute dislike of me.'

Emily chuckled. 'You are like me. A bit of Irish are you?'

'Half and half.'

'Generosity is a good weapon. My mother used to say, "Don't get mad, get even", and I always do in the end.'

'I can imagine.' He was grinning. 'I've heard a lot about you.'

'I'll ring Emma tonight if you think she's better.'

'Doc said she's walking about in a dressing-gown so she can answer the phone now.'

'I enjoyed talking to you. When the baby comes, bring her and Eileen down to the sea. It will do them both good, and you can use Emma's cottage.'

'Her, did you say?'

'Of course. You'll have a beautiful daughter.'

'Thanks very much!' Mick said to the now silent phone. 'Bang goes my train set.'

He reflected on the neat piles he'd made of clothes and personal belongings and was glad that Emma Sykes had no need to see them. The stripped beds and half-empty cupboards seemed to him to look like the result of pillage.

'It's like dividing the spoils of a robbery,' he said to Arthur who came in to help. 'I'll stay until tomorrow so I'll still need the bed in the small room but I don't know what to do about the bedclothes. Could Judy take them and wash them and then keep them?'

'No trouble. She'll be pleased. Good bed linen isn't easy to come by these days even if it is off-ration, like clothes now. Even what they choose to call double bed sheets are skimpy and my feet stick out as we can't tuck the sheets in properly.'

'Ask her to come in and take a pile of stuff. Some of it is good pre-war quality without the utility kite mark label. I don't see why Mrs Hammond should have the first pick and the doc said to make sure you both had something for all your trouble.'

'You're paying me over the odds for caretaking. I'd have done that for nothing, Mick. It will be interesting and give me something to do other than gardening and odd jobs.'

'Money isn't the issue. When I go,

we'll all feel safer with you in charge here.' Mick regarded him cautiously as if he didn't want to hurt his pride. 'The lawyer asked who would be here as we'd need someone and I said that you would be in charge until after the sale. He asked if you did this often as he could do with someone new on his books who could be trusted.'

Arthur blinked. 'Not really my line, but better than temporary jobs in offices. I'd be on my own and be my own boss, and I could take a job now and then when I felt like it.'

'Take his number and say I sent you, if you decide to do it.'

'I wouldn't want any clothes,' Judy said when she looked at the piles on the bed.

'Take the linen and towels, and this.' Mick said firmly.

'I couldn't!' Judy smoothed the fur jacket with tremulous hands.

'You could and you will. The doc would want you to have something decent and Mrs Sykes wouldn't wear it.' He thrust it into her hands. 'I feel like Father Christmas but the best bit will be when I kindly give that lot to Mrs Hammond!'

'If she thinks you've been rude to her

she'll refuse to take it.'

'Not her! She'll hate my guts and I'll not expect a kiss of gratitude but she'll grab whatever I give her.'

'We'll get this lot out of the way,' Arthur said. 'Go on, pick it up! You can wear that when we have the British Legion do next week.' He warmed to the task. 'Mind if I look in the shed to see if there's a decent gardening fork?'

'I looked and there's a lot of old junk but a fairly new lawn mower if that's any use to you.'

'I'll have a look.'

Mick glanced at his watch. 'I think I'll go back this afternoon. There's no point in hanging about here. I do have a job in London and I want to see Eileen. I'll drop the keys through your letter box, Arthur and you can take it from there. Mrs Hammond will be here in half an hour and then I want to go home.'

He opened the note that the lawyer had written stating the facts of Mr Dewar's will and that Mrs Hammond had no right to take anything except through the good will of the owners' representative, and when she arrived he showed it to her.

Mick ignored her white-faced rage and

pointed to the piles of clothes. 'You are welcome to that lot,' he said and waited in silence while she struggled to her car several times with armfuls of clothes, as Mick wanted to keep the Dewar suitcases for his own use on the way to London, the bag of shoes and her own suitcase, heavy with china plates and cups. She slammed the car door and drove away without a word.

Mick felt as if he needed a shower after she left, to wash away her malignance and the aura of sadness in the house. He checked each room and left without a backward glance after ringing for the cab. He bundled in the cases that contained everything that Emily Darwen had said wouldn't offend Emma, then was driven to the station where he put the now considerable amount of luggage in the guard's van.

'How are you going to manage that lot at the other end?' asked the cab driver, who had bought a one-penny platform ticket so that he could help with the luggage onto the train.

'I'll get a porter and I can carry two suitcases,' Mick replied. His spirits lifted as the train passed through Bath and he saw the green hills beyond the sunlit stone city. I couldn't stay at that house another day, he decided, and his thoughts flew ahead to Eileen and the doc and the good, warm home they had in Kensington.

Two porters stood idly on the platform at Victoria Station and Mick beckoned. 'I've a load of stuff here Mate,' he said. 'I had help in Bristol but I can't manage this on my own.'

'Turned over a gaff?' one said, grinning.

'Just a family funeral and I got out before the vultures took over.'

'Know what you mean.'

'What's going on over there?'

Men in army uniform hefting kitbags and greatcoats stood around smoking. Mick saw the blue berets of the United Nations and the hair at the back of his neck prickled.

'Korea,' the porter said shortly. 'I'm glad to be out of it this time.'

Mick put down the two cases he was carrying, reached over to the trolley and grabbed the long walking umbrella from the pack of sundries balanced on the other cases 'You don't need that. We've had no rain for days. It's hot out there,' the porter grumbled as the bundle sagged and he had to tighten the strap holding it together. Mick began to limp. 'A war wound?' The man was immediately helpful and pulled the remaining luggage onto the second trolley.

'Leg suddenly giving me gyp. Thanks. I'll need both trolleys as I can't carry anything just now.'

With his practised limp, Mick followed the two porters along the platform past the soldiers to the cab rank outside. He leaned heavily on the umbrella.

'Grade!' Mick turned, and as he told Eileen later, your heart really does come into your mouth! 'It *is* Grade? Still got that limp, I see.'

'Mustn't grumble, Sir. Got a nice desk job now and I hardly need this any more,' he said bravely.

'Good luck. I could do with you here, but I can see it's impossible. That's our transport,' the CO added hastily and went swiftly to join his fellow officers.

'Good luck to you too, Sir,' Mick replied and watched the blue berets board the train.

He was smiling when the cab arrived in Kensington. He saw the bay trees by the front door, dark green and glossy leaved and his heart was light.

'You're back early,' Mrs Coster said accusingly. 'Mind that wet patch. I've just washed it.'

'Now I know I'm home! Is the guvnor about?'

'Up in the office with Sister. She's ever so much better and having more of an appetite, and as for your Eileen, she never stops eating!'

'I'll bring the bags in later. We left them in the porch,' he explained and Mick took the stairs two at a time, to the office.

'Good to see you,' Paul said warmly. 'Last patient gone and Eileen is making tea, so we can all have some together and you can tell us the news.'

'Did I hear Mick?' Emma came from the consulting room, beaming at him. She looked pale and had lost a little weight but her eyes were clear and she had more strength in her voice. 'Help Eileen make the tea,' she suggested. 'Take your time as she'll want to say hello and tell you all about our flu.'

'Right, Sister.' Mick hurried away and five minutes later returned carrying the tray, with Eileen following him and looking delighted to have him back with her.

'Are you feeling strong enough for this?' Paul asked gently.

Emma nodded. 'I wept any tears over my family years ago and now it all seems unreal or as if this had happened to another person with whom I am not really involved. I ought to feel guilty but I was glad I was ill and couldn't go to the funeral.'

'Just as well,' Mick said bluntly. 'I'd have hated you to be there, Sister. It was no skin off my nose to act for you. I enjoyed it and I managed to see the funny side quite often. I met the neighbours, Judy and Arthur. They remembered you but said your mother kept you away from them because you seemed to like them.'

'That's true.'

Gradually Mick told them of what had happened and Emma shook her head several times as if she knew it was all true but couldn't believe it. She laughed when Mick gave a heavily embroidered account of his meeting with Mrs Hammond and Eileen urged him to tell them more.

'I'll bring the bags into the hall,' he said at last. 'No hurry to go through them until you feel up to it, Sister. One case is packed with things for Miss Darwen and your other aunt, so that can stay until you go to the Island again.'

'Will they want anything from that house?' asked Emma, uncertainly. 'Neither Aunt Emily nor Aunt Janey shared her taste in anything.'

'I spoke to your aunt and read her a list and she found a few items on it that were hers by right and some silver belonging to your Aunt Janey that came to her from her first marriage. It happened to find it's way to your mother who conveniently forgot she had it.'

'Oh dear, you make my mother sound like a criminal.'

'Not that, Emma.' Paul was firm. 'She was a very unhappy woman who gave no love and then wondered why people didn't want her. Such people grasp at material things that they can take from others, hoping to fill a gap and convince themselves that they have some hold on people, usually their families. If you had remained in Bristol she would have used you and expected more and more until she made you feel guilty that she was unhappy in spite of all your efforts. I meet this a lot and when I see their sons or daughters in that situation I try to break that bond and make them look outward, but it is sometimes impossible.'

'I've known that for years,' Emma accepted. 'But I never thought of it as a clinical condition.' She looked sad.

'I'll help you unpack tomorrow,' Mick offered. 'I'll bring one bag at a time up to your rooms and leave you to sort it out.'

'What would we do without you?' Emma was moved.

'You nearly had to. I had a narrow squeak at Victoria. There was I carrying two heavy cases when I saw some blue berets. I had a feeling that my old CO was with them and I had to think fast so I dropped the cases, grabbed an umbrella and did my limp just in time, as he saw me and recognised me.'

They all laughed. 'You must have caught a bit of Aunt Emily's psychic power of premonition,' Emma said at last. 'What's the matter, Mick? You seem worried.'

'She isn't really, is she? You know, she hasn't the power to go telling the future?'

'I didn't believe it either but I do now,' Paul offered.

'Flippin' Hell!'

'Language,' Eileen said.

'Did she tell you something on the

phone?' asked Emma.

'Of course not.'

'You are a *fibber,* Mick Grade,' Eileen accused him.

'She just said that when we have the baby she wants us to take her down to the Island for a holiday and stay in Sister's cottage. That's all she said.'

Eileen blushed. 'That was kind.' Then the light dawned and she almost shrieked. 'She said *her!* We're going to have a baby girl, Mick.'

'You mustn't believe all she says,' Emma began, but it was too late.

'I knew I should make the clothes pink.' Eileen was jubilant.

'Come on Eileen. I want my supper and it's time that Sister had a rest from you yacketing on about the baby. It was only a slip of the tongue so don't you go believing that rubbish or you might be disappointed when we have a strapping boy.'

'You look a bit weary,' Paul said when the couple had gone down to their flat, happily arguing and obviously contented.

'Relieved more than weary but I feel that I can let go now. I was a bit tense when Mick was doing what I thought was my duty, but now I know I couldn't have

205

stayed in that house again. I could never have faced Mrs Hammond either as our dislike was mutual and she was a real bully.'

Paul nodded. 'It takes a bully to dominate a person who mistakes it for caring,' Paul said. 'That's probably why they were so close.' He laughed. 'Mick is really wonderful with people like that.'

'Yes, I saw him in action on the ward. He could cool a situation between the men and yet not lose their respect; but he's not an angel! He's a bit of a con artist, too,' she admitted. 'He fooled a lot of people into getting our supplies through much more quickly than we could have done and over the telephone; they often thought he must be a very senior person on the hospital staff. I'll write to Bea tomorrow. She'll be enchanted when I tell her how he managed in Bristol.'

'Don't make her too nostalgic, Emma. Half of her wants to be back here and even though Dwight will not go to Korea, she is anxious about the situation as they are very close to the White House in every way. She can't share a lot of beliefs the Americans hold. So many are besotted by MacArthur and she takes a different view and finds it hard to keep quiet.'

'Is he a danger?'

'Bea's father says so but admits that he is necessary so long as he doesn't have grandiose ideas about invading China, just across the border from Korea. That would mean a third world war in his estimation and we would be dragged into a war that doesn't concern us as a nation.'

'We are sending men with the United Nations contingent,' Emma reminded him.

'A peacekeeping force.'

'Do you really believe it could stop there?'

Paul spoke quietly. 'MacArthur said that Japan was finished as a manufacturing nation, but now that supplies from America are difficult to transport to Korea, he is permitting the rebuilding of factories to produce war machines and ships. The Japanese lack the ability as yet to design new goods but are quick to copy whatever is available, such as the prefabricated ship parts that America made during the war. I think he may have given them the power to start again very quickly, and if the Americans have the guns and MacArthur's arrogance, they will use them.'

'That's what Bea says and Dwight agrees

in private but as a part of the establishment he has to be circumspect.'

The house phone trilled. 'Eileen fancies fish and chips so if I go, do you want any?'

'Yes please Mick, two lots,' Paul laughed. 'Trust Mick to deal with practicalities. This evening, fish and chips seem more realistic than General MacArthur, Korea and the whole Japanese question.'

## Chapter Eleven

'This room hasn't changed, except for the bed.' Dwight looked less like a high-ranking American air force officer now that he was with the White House in Washington, and on this trip to England, more like a prosperous businessman at leisure. His clothes were well cut but decidedly American and his shoes were of thick leather with squared toes over bright socks.

'You took the four-poster to Texas,' Emma reminded him. 'When we knew you were coming we had to buy a bed in a hurry to cover the bare patch left on the carpet where the other bed had been, and give you somewhere to sleep if you wanted to come to us and not to a grand hotel. This is it, like it or not.'

'I love it.' He smoothed the brass knobs on the bedstead and regarded the crimson velour cover with admiration.

'Bea will just love this.'

'Will she follow you soon?' Emma asked eagerly.

'Not just now, as I'll be back home directly.' He saw her disappointment. 'This trip was scheduled so quickly there wasn't time to make arrangements for the twins and you know how picky my wife can be about the twins. Bea refuses to leave them with just anyone who can spoon oatmeal into two small demanding mouths.'

'What happened to the dear dependable English nanny?'

'On leave,' he said laconically and Emma sensed that he was lying. 'Where did you buy this heap? It's really something but I don't know what.'

'Mick bought it in the Portobello Road. He saw it there and Paul went to check and thought it would fit in nicely, with a fresh mattress.'

'Bea wanted a few pictures, so I'll start on this one.' He produced a very expensive camera and took a photograph of the bedroom, then the office, the consulting rooms and the front of the house with Paul and Emma at the door flanked by the two bay trees.

After lunch he changed into uniform and looked serious. 'My car will be here in five minutes. I shall be late back so can I have a key? See you at breakfast.' He kissed Emma and hurried to the front hall.

'Is he all right? He seems edgy.'

'Nothing bad,' Paul reassured her. 'They have a meeting of Chiefs of Staff and he is liaising with the various services over here. His godfather is involved and so they asked Dwight to come over.' He laughed. 'The General is convinced that any relative of his would starve here so we have another big parcel that will delight your greedy heart and send Eileen into ecstasies.'

'*My* greedy heart? So you don't want the goodies?'

'Have to build you up. You've lost weight.'

Emma sighed. 'Eileen hasn't! Her time is going on and she will be due in four weeks' time.'

Paul hugged her. 'Not still fretting?'

'Not really. In a way I feel excited and I am looking forward to having a baby in the house, but I shall be jealous if I'm not very careful.'

'Rubbish. You haven't a jealous nerve in your body.'

'Does Dwight know that?'

'What do you mean? You've never been jealous of Bea having the twins.'

'She didn't telephone last week on the day she promised and Dwight rang at a time when I wasn't available and said she had a cold and was asleep.' She looked at Paul as if he shared some plot with Dwight and Bea. 'When would Bea pass up a call to me unless she was at death's door? I know she isn't or Dwight would be there fussing over her, regardless of any international situation.'

'These things happen without there being any sinister undertones.'

'Dwight has made sure since he arrived this morning that he isn't left alone with me and I know it isn't because he fancies me and can't trust himself now that Bea isn't here,' she said dryly. 'Also, I don't know how he gets on with the diplomats, as he's a bad liar.'

211

Paul sighed. 'I told him to tell you.'

'Tell me what?'

'You'd better wait until he comes back.'

'And bite my nails up to the elbows, wondering? Tell me, Paul. Is Bea pregnant again? That is the only excuse I can think of that would prevent her from coming over with Dwight.'

'Yes, she is pregnant and dreaded having to tell you.'

'I'm OK. Other people's babies don't worry me any more ... I think.' Emma burst into tears and he held her close, smoothing her hair and feeling totally inadequate.

'Paul?' She made a positive effort to dry her eyes. 'I've been a selfish bitch. I've slopped around feeling weak and sorry for myself long enough. We haven't even made love since before I had the flu. Have I been selfish, turning away from you at night? I seem to have thought of nobody but myself for weeks and wasted far too much time thinking of what might have been with my mother if we'd been closer.' She gave a wan smile. 'I'm glad I know about Bea. It was the shock I needed. Life goes on. I mustn't look back and I have responsibilities. I have to look after Eileen soon and I must ring Bea and tell her I'm delighted; and so I am.'

'Good girl,' he said quietly. He chuckled. 'Dwight will be very relieved to know he can come in safely and not be met by a white-faced girl in tears. He'll find talking to the powers-that-be at the Foreign Office a doddle compared to that.'

'If you don't need me in the consulting room, I'll have a chat with Eileen and decide what we can make for Dwight. He'll have eaten before he comes back but we know Dwight well enough to know that he'll demand food at midnight if any is available! The General sent a large chicken and lots of cans of food, so maybe a pie made with the rougher bits of the chicken and some ham will fill a gap and I can make a chicken casserole with the rest for tomorrow.'

'Shut the kitchen door while you cook or my next patient will go mad if he smells enticing food. His wife makes him eat not just vegetarian food but the weirdest selection of plants. I think he's slightly poisoned and his depression might have something to do with starvation. She collects so-called mushrooms which sounds ominous.'

'I'll send up some nice milky coffee and biscuits. Do you think he'd like a sausage roll?' She asked mischievously.

'Not if you want to break up his marriage. Once he tastes good food, who knows what might happen in his home? It could mean mutiny! Coffee by all means but no sausage roll.'

'Why don't you put him on a diet that includes fish and eggs but forbids fungi. It's too soon to include red meat but some protein might help.'

Paul reflected on her suggestion. 'Could you compile a light diet similar to a post-operative one? He does need something like that as he has stomach pains after some of his wife's culinary disasters and dreads the idea of surgery. That's when he has mild panic attacks, thinks he's going mad and sinks deeper into depression. He said that her latest fad is young bracken in the tightly curled stage as she heard it was like asparagus, but it's slightly poisonous taken in large quantities and at this time of the year is no longer tender and innocuous, but too coarse to eat and be safe.'

'I'll make up a diet and ask Mick to type it out on our very impressive headed notepaper. You could say that he must stick to it or you'll have to refer him to the surgeons. Even his wife must take that seriously. Hint at possible allergies.' She smiled.

'What's funny.'

'I think *he* needs a good meal and *she* needs the psychiatrist.'

'Perhaps you should allow the aroma of chicken pie to reach him and stir his digestive juices, but that would be too cruel.'

Eileen cut up the chicken, put the drumsticks and thighs aside for another meal and cubed the rest of the meat with a tin of ham to make pie filling. She protested only weakly when Emma insisted that they could make the filling do for one large pie and a small one for Mick and Eileen, and put the carcase in a large pot with onions, carrots, parsley and thyme, with a lot of potatoes and a Maggi tomato cube to simmer for two hours to make soup.

Emma rolled out the pastry as if the even strokes could calm her inner feelings and found pleasure in crimping the edges of the pies and seeing them neat and symmetrical.

'You are so artistic, Sister. Is there

anything you can't do well?'

Emma tried to laugh. 'As Mick would say, I can't strike a match on a bar of soap.'

'He's awful!' Eileen's voice was full of affection. 'Nice to have Mr Dwight here again. I wonder why he didn't bring the family? He had every comfort in the plane they used to bring him here, or so Mick said. I'd like to see the twins again and I miss them all.'

Emma took a deep breath and thought, I won't cry. I will be strong and keep calm. She looked at Eileen's swollen belly and almost ran to the deep larder, counted to twenty and took slow breaths before turning back into the kitchen with a dish she didn't need.

'She couldn't come this time,' she heard her own calm voice say. 'Bea is pregnant again.'

'Oh, Sister! How lovely.' Eileen glanced at the pale face and the tension in Emma's soft mouth. 'I wish it was you. You never talk about it so I suppose you don't want children, but you would be a wonderful mother, Sister.'

'I doubt if we can have children.'

Eileen looked confused. 'Sorry if I said

something out of turn but look at us. We had been married for a long time and tried to have a baby and we had almost given up hope when it happened, suddenly. It will surely happen to you Sister. Mark my words, Nature couldn't be that cruel to you and the doc.'

'Nature is very cruel,' Emma said quietly. 'What can we have for pudding?'

'There's enough milk for junket to go with the raspberries.' Eileen looked at her sharply and talked of food and patients, Mick and Korea, and avoided mentioning babies.

Paul had an emergency with a patient who had a persecution complex and it was late before he had him admitted to a secure hospital for tests as he suspected that the tertiary stage of syphilis was to blame for his condition. It was a long time before the patient could be made to see the sense in being examined further and Paul sedated him.

The ambulance left at last and Emma took sandwiches and coffee to the office where Paul was slumped in a leather chair, drained of energy.

'Dwight rang to say he'd be home much earlier than he thought possible, so I offered him food here and we can eat the pie with him, but you must be hungry so the sandwiches will fill a gap.' Emma smiled. 'It's all right. I congratulated him on the new coming event,' she said lightly. 'Poor Dwight was so relieved that I knew and I wasn't upset. He must think I'm a monster devoured by envy, but now he can feel relaxed about showing us the hundreds of photographs of the twins he must have in his luggage.'

Dwight was tired and accepted a glass of wine with gratitude. 'More difficult listening to a bunch of armchair politicians saying a load of crap than having the twins on my own for half a day and that's saying something, believe me.'

'I suppose you have to watch them every minute at that age,' Paul said.

'Every *half* minute,' Dwight retorted. 'I'll have grey hair soon.' He drained his glass and held it out for more, then withheld it when Paul brought the bottle over. 'Better eat first as I'm empty and I might talk too much if I drink another glass before a meal.'

'You, talk too much? You have to be joking,' Emma said dryly. 'Sit up and we'll have the pie we made specially for you today, so don't tell us of the wonderful food you had at the last ambassadorial dinner in Washington.'

'This is the tops! You should be head cook at the White House. It would bring peace on earth for all time.' He sighed. 'That was real good. Half the world's tragedies are caused by dyspepsia.'

'Two much German sauerkraut and Japanese seaweed?' suggested Emma.

'I told Bea to ring,' Dwight said. 'About now if she can get through.' He grinned. 'I'll answer the phone as she'll want to know if you are still talking to her.'

'I'll make coffee from the General's lovely coffee beans. You should come over more often, Dwight.'

'That's my girl now!' As the phone rang, Dwight almost ran to take the call and said, 'Leave the coffee or let Paul make it. You have to talk.' He lifted the receiver. 'Hi Honey!'

Emma watched his face grow gentle. 'You *did?*' He chuckled and glanced at Emma. 'Guess what? She threw up four times today so now she knows it's true.' He listened again and nodded. 'It's OK. When did you ever doubt her? Here she is and I'll say goodnight; I'm bushed. Coffee and bed in something you never dreamed about, Hon. A brass bedstead with knobs on!'

'Bea? how is my fertile friend?' Emma said.

'I feel terrible! You realise it's morning here? And what happens to preggie women in the mornings? I think it's over for the day now or I couldn't have phoned. It's not nice to be sick when your beloved husband says he loves you.'

'Obviously he does still love you,' Emma said mildly.

'It's too early to know what is happening in there but if it's twins again you must have them!' Her laugh was almost a sob. 'Maybe I have to be brood mare for your children, Duckie.' Suddenly she was serious. 'I wish I was, or that we could do this together. We've done everything together for years now and it isn't fair. I felt so guilty when I knew, that I wept. We didn't intend it to happen again so soon.'

'*C'est la vie.* Paul and I are used to the idea now and I shall have a baby in the house soon. Eileen has swelled up nicely and looks blooming. I am setting up as a universal aunt.'

'Don't give me that. Why not holler and

tell me you hate me?'

'I don't. The past few weeks have made me think carefully about what Paul and I have and what is impossible. When my mother died I knew that my life was due for a change, not that we had anything to give each other in recent years, but now I have to look forward and take what is good, rejecting false sentiment and nostalgia for things that were never really there.'

'Stop crying, Duckie. No, let it out, Dewar! I'm crying too. We've shed tears together before now. Remember the night of the firebombs when we got drunk? Remember the night when Maeve was killed and Sister Cary admitted that she'd had a fiancé killed in the first lot and really had a heart under that icy front?'

'Don't.'

'It seemed as if the end of the world was coming, but here we are.' Her voice cleared. 'I need you, Emma. Last night I wanted you here, laughing with the twins and teasing Dwight and me. I was lonely without my dear insulting husband and I longed to come over the pond to see you.'

'I miss you too.' Emma tried to sound

cheerful. 'We'll have to wait until your baby arrives before you come over here, now.'

'I might manage it before then if Dwight can find a pressurised plane when the obstetrician says it's safe to fly.'

'We'll be ready anytime. Eileen and Mick are wonderful, especially Mick. If you bring the twins after Eileen has her baby we shall have a full nursery. What a good thing the walls here are thick!' She told Bea about his trip to Bristol and his determination not to go to Korea and when they put down their phones they were both smiling.

Outside the office, Dwight sat cross-legged on the floor, waving a big handkerchief. 'Any mopping up to do?' he asked laconically. He stood to put an arm round her shoulders and they went into the kitchen for coffee and cake.

Paul ignored the tear-stains and noticed only the smile. 'I take it that Bea is well,' he enquired. 'Had a good chat?'

'That call would cost a roustabout a week's pay,' Dwight grumbled.

'What a good thing that Bea married a rich man.'

'It was worth it to know that I can go

home without Bea throwing me out as a thoughtless moron who didn't sign the peace. I gather they've had a few tears and a bit of blue birds over the white cliffs.'

'You listened!'

'Of course I listened. What gives with Mick and the war? You'll have to learn to speak up. I didn't get that bit.'

'Bed,' Emma said firmly at last. 'That is if we can sleep after all that wonderful coffee.'

'I shall crash out. I want to wake up and see a dozen small bright suns winking at me from the bed posts. The twins will love them, but probably think they are candy!'

'That doesn't matter. You took the other bed and you aren't robbing us of this one.' Paul sounded amused.

'Cheapskate! Goodnight and God bless.' Dwight put a hand on Emma's shoulder, bent to kiss her cheek and waved a languid hand in goodnight.

'Bea seemed very close tonight.' Emma was thoughtful. 'Have you ever felt that someone was looking after you? I have felt Aunt Emily close to me lately as if she really has taken the place of my mother. She was already that long ago but now she can let herself feel the link more strongly and it comes through.'

'Come to bed. It's been an exciting day. Were you very disturbed when you spoke to Bea?'

Emma leaned against him as they went to their bedroom. 'No, that call was a catharsis and I feel very peaceful.'

'I'm glad.' He turned her face to his and kissed her with great tenderness, growing to deep passion. Smiling, she undressed and slipped between the sheets naked and Paul rested his head on her breasts.

'Happy?' he asked.

'Very. We are what matters, Paul.' Her arms went round his body and held him close. She was wide awake and throbbing with the need for his love in the quiet moonlit room.

## Chapter Twelve

'I'm glad you came.' Emily Darwen picked up the smallest case and followed Emma and Paul into the cottage. 'Wilf had to push a bird's nest out of the chimney and lay a trap for mice but he thinks he's got them all now. Only one family, he says, the birds have gone and you don't need the fire this weather.'

'He's so good to us,' Emma said.

'Got a very soft spot for you both but grumbles that you can't expect a cottage to be free of vermin if it's left empty for months on end.'

'It was wonderful to see the ferry and to know we were coming here.' Emma took a deep breath. 'It's fine where we live but the air here is quite different and I could smell hay on a cart coming from along the Blackwater Road. Now, I can't wait to pick some really fresh vegetables.'

'There's a better selection in my garden. Wilf tidies up here but he plants mostly at the house so that produce is there when I want anything. George put in some raspberry canes earlier this year, and the potatoes, as Wilf isn't as young as he was and his boy has gone to the boatyard in Cowes and only comes home at weekends.' Emily sniffed. 'We think he has a girl there but he never lets on. He could come home every night on the train if he wanted to, not take a room over there during the week.'

Emma silently congratulated the lad,

who could easily have become a farm labourer under his father's thumb and never leave the farmhouse.

'There must be plenty of boys willing to earn something here. Enough out of work after the war,' Paul reflected.

'We don't do badly. Dr Sutton has one lad each day and another for two days a week and I have him for another two, but we need Wilf. He has to see that things get done. He's still the best workman and knows a weed from a plant!'

'I'll drive round to the house,' Paul suggested. 'We have a heavy case for you from Bristol, so I'll put it in your conservatory for unpacking, if it's not too hot there. We seem about to have a thunderstorm, as if this heat wasn't enough. I'll leave you two there and come back to open a few more windows and unpack while you have a good long chat. The air is so still I want to get the stuff out of the car before it rains. Just look at that coppery sky.'

'Have a cup of tea first,' Emily begged after Paul had dropped them at the house. 'No need to unpack a lot. I want to hear all Emma's news.' Her dark eyes gleamed with pleasure and an underlying excitement.

'I'll be back in ten minutes,' he promised. 'I'd better bring the car to take Emma back in the dry.'

Heavy spots of rain began to fall slowly, making dark circles like pennies dropped in the dust and sending up an acrid scent as the thirsty dry earth drank the moisture.

'You said that George was here?' asked Emma when Paul had gone back to the cottage after leaving the heavy case with Emily in the small morning room, as the glassed-in conservatory was almost tropical.

Emily nodded. 'George likes to come here on his own for a day when he is staying with Janey and Alex and little Clive. Janey thinks that he needs to be here to recoup a little without a boisterous boy demanding his every minute. He loves Clive dearly but this place has a few memories and he always looks better for a day digging or walking over the Downs. I think he wonders if there's going to be another war out East that will affect him.'

'Aunt Janey is a very understanding mother considering that she has the responsibility of looking after Clive all the time and must enjoy George's company when he has leave.'

'She thanks God every day for giving her a child to look after as George was her only one from her first marriage and she didn't have any with Alex, so she can afford to be understanding.'

'Is George ... has he found someone?'

'There's talk of a Wren officer whom he sees, but it may be nothing. You've a lot to answer for, my girl. He still thinks of you and Janey knows it. She's like George. She lost the love of her life too when he was lost at sea in that terrible submarine, but she married his best friend and is very happy, so she hopes that after a period of recovery, George will do the same.'

'You forgot to put the kettle on,' Emma replied, adding firmly, 'George has come to terms with his crush on me.'

'Maybe. I'll make the tea and we can turn out this case and see what treasures your mother passed on. Clear that table and put a cloth on it.'

'It won't upset you?'

'Not one little bit. I've got over the shock of her death and I'm curious to know what she had of mine!'

'Amazing what one case can hold,' Paul

said from the doorway. 'As if that wasn't enough, here is another box with silver and dishes. Don't bother to drag yourselves away. I'll pour my own tea!'

'I remember this.' Emma picked up a blue and white dish. 'We never used it and I wanted to bring it out one Christmas for our Christmas dinner but Mother said I'd break it and it was valuable. She put it away and I never saw it again.' Emma ran a finger down the ornamental indented runs that led to a shallow dip at one end so that fat from a large joint, a goose or a duck or even a suckling pig, could be drained free of grease and the juices from the meat could be gathered to help make an enriched gravy.

'What about this?'

Emma shook her head over ornaments and pictures that had been in the Bristol house but held no memories for her. 'Why were these things on Mick's list for you?'

'When he read out that list I knew they were either my things or came from our mother. Clare kept quiet about the things she had from the house on the Mall and I wondered where they were. I must give some to Janey and that vase was definitely hers, one that George's father, Clive, gave her when he was posted abroad.'

'What's that?' Emma saw that Emily was moved, under her disciplined calm. She watched her aunt unwrap the tissue paper that Mick had carefully put round the picture and laid flat in the bottom of the case and for the first time, saw the portrait of her own grandmother, an enlarged sepia-coloured photograph of a woman sitting in a chair against a wooden trellis and a huge aspidistra plant on a stand, the usual background favoured by Victorian photographers. 'Your mother?'

Emily nodded. 'You must have this to keep, Emma.'

'She was lovely.' Emma stared at the oval face with the dark eyes and scraped back thick dark hair. 'Did she always wear a cameo brooch? It goes well with that lacy high collar and dark dress. Do you have the brooch?'

Emma picked up the linen bag in which Mick had put the trinkets, but Emily took it away from her. 'It isn't in there. We'll go through that in a minute.' She seemed to be in a dream. 'This picture was taken when she still had it. She must have been quite young, but after we were born. It was done before she was very ill.'

'When did she lose the cameo?'

'She didn't lose it. She gave it away to a gypsy woman who was kind to her. So much is a mystery to me, as I was young and took no notice of what was happening. I was there when Mother nearly died in childbirth but your Uncle Sidney knew more about that time as he was friendly with the gypsy boys down at Wootton and Mother used to go down there with him.'

'And Uncle Sidney is dead so we'll never know.'

'Don't look sad. Keep the picture after I've had it framed.' Emily looked pensive. 'She would have loved you. She loved children and was happy to have a large family, until she nearly died.'

Emma felt tears under her eyelids and blinked furiously. Why didn't you pass on those genes? she wanted to demand. She gulped and looked again at the face and saw a calm sadness that hinted at dignified resignation in the expression. 'You have her dark hair and eyes.'

'We all did,' Emily remembered. 'You have the look of her, too.'

'I can see that,' Paul said.

'I wish I'd known her. Can you really bear to part with this, Aunt Emily?'

'As I haven't seen it for years and thought it had gone, I can pass it over to you with pleasure.'

'You have the original small picture in this album.' Paul turned the yellowing leaves at the beginning of a book with oval cardboard settings for photographs and he smiled. 'What a tiny waist you had, Emily.'

'Where?' Emma looked over his shoulder at a group of young women dressed in long dark skirts and high-necked shirt blouses and wide straw hats decorated with artificial flowers.

'You were all pretty.' Emma was fascinated. 'That's you, looking shy and that's Aunt Janey, plump and sweet-looking and that's my mother.' Silently, she studied each face and saw that even then Clare Darwen had an imperious, discontented expression and a hat that tried to outdo the others as a stuffed bird sat among her flowers. 'Who was this?'

'Your Aunt Liz, as usual copying Clare and eating anything that came her way. She was never fat but had a big appetite. Even in the picture she's eating an apple.'

Emma giggled. 'What happened to the boys?'

'They never liked being snapped. Sidney took that one as he was good at it and was the artistic one of the family.'

'Look at the rest later,' Paul suggested.

'Yes, let's get rid of this case first and I want to go through the other pictures with you.' Emily put a small clock on the mantelpiece after winding it and then shaking it vigorously. 'It didn't work years ago so I don't expect miracles now. I'll take it in to be cleaned and see if the spring's broken. Janey might like it, and when you've seen the rest of the album, I'll save it to show her as there are lots of pictures of her and her first husband in there.'

Emma put down the thick book with reluctance. The people in there were suddenly real! She had relatives who had come to life through the fading pictures and she yearned to have known them better and to have shared in the life of a large and vital family.

'I'll buy another album and perhaps Emma can have what you can spare.' Paul had noticed the reluctance that Emma felt as she handed the book over until Emily would decide to go through it later.

'There's a man in Newport who copies

old photographs and tints them to bring them up to date. Very good and a lot of people like to have their families remembered in that way so he does well out of it. His father started with photographs of men killed in the first war, often making them better-looking than in the original pictures. His son carried on building up a good business in the last war and does some very nice work.' She chuckled. 'There were a lot of heartbroken girls with dolled up pictures of their American boyfriends who loved them and left them and are now settled back in the USA with their wives.'

'Let me know where to find him. I'll have some copies done.' Paul smiled and glanced at Emma's head bent over a picture of the River Medina with the Victorian cranes on the wharf. 'Janey will want some for George and we would like a lot of those pictures.'

'George?' Emma looked up sharply.

'She was his grandmother too,' he pointed out. 'Clive might want to see what his forebears looked like and even want to pass them on if he has children.'

It all came back to that, Emma thought resentfully. Nobody allowed her to forget the next generation and she had nothing to pass on, or at least there was no person to receive her possessions or genes.

'Of course, and Aunt Janey will want her own share,' was all she said.

'Eileen is nearly due so you were wise to come here for a few days before she's delivered as I don't know when you'll fit in a visit after that, for a long time,' Emily said.

'It was a sudden decision,' Paul remarked. 'Emma wanted to see you and give you these things and I'm sorry we caught you unawares, coming here as soon as Dwight left for Washington.' Paul grinned. 'That's unless you knew we were coming.'

'Cheeky thing!' But Emily didn't deny that she had a feeling that they might come to the Island, and Wilf had said he had to look over the cottage in a hurry, the previous week.

'Shall we go for a walk?' Paul asked.

'Later, when it cools off a little.' Emma moved restlessly. 'Thunder would be nice to break up this heavy weather. I'd rather drive out to West Wight. If there's any cool air, that will be the place to find it.'

Paul nodded and she was aware that he

was watching her closely. Both Paul and Emily seemed cool but she was too warm. It wasn't a rise in temperature as she was completely over the flu and felt better than she'd done for ages.

'The rain came to nothing. We can go if that's what you want but there's going to be a downpour soon. We could be caught in it on the way to Freshwater and it can blow a gale along the Military Road.'

As if to prove Paul's point, the skies darkened and the earth gave up its scent to the early drops.

'Help me pick the vegetables, Emma, and Paul can give me a hand covering up my plants.'

They hurried into the garden. Emma cut a cabbage and Emily picked runner beans while Paul lifted the huge earthenware pots and turned them upside down to cover the delicate leaves of the Christmas roses.

'You have bigger pots this year.' Emma peered at the soft leaves.

'I'll have a nice few to pick after Christmas,' Emily smiled. 'The first good harvest, and they will look nice in that little vase that looks like a basket.'

'Harvest is usually in the autumn. "Season of mists and mellow fruitfulness," and all those marrows!'

'This harvest will be very good. With everything considered I think it will be one of the best.'

'You mean Bea?' There it was again. The earth would produce the white waxy flowers close to Emily's heart and Bea would be fruitful once more.

'Bea too,' was her reply. 'Here it comes!' They ran back to the house, Emily trailing after the younger couple. They picked tomatoes in the conservatory and the rain lashed down on the glass roof. 'It sounds like lead shot!' Paul marvelled.

In the open doorway, Emma raised her face to the rain and her hair was wet. 'That's better. I've gone off the idea of Yarmouth today so let me cook supper.'

'It's almost ready. I've cooked a piece of nice gammon. You make a parsley sauce and I'll do the beans and potatoes.'

Emma eyed the bacon joint that was still in the cooking liquor, waiting to be heated up again. 'It's huge. You did know we were coming!'

'I thought you might find it convenient just now before things start happening. Common sense,' she added defensively, then hesitated. 'We'll go through the album tonight and Paul can order the copies in the morning but I think you'd be more comfortable in your own home now, so get back there later tomorrow. You don't want to rush around.'

'You think that Eileen will be early?'

'You ought to go back,' Emily repeated.

'I'm glad we came but it's much too short a visit. However, Eileen comes first and I promised to drive her to the hospital as soon as they want her there. Mick might get a bit rash if he has to drive. He's the world's best pillar of strength in the normal way but most fathers-in-waiting are a bit fraught.'

Emily nodded. 'Quite right.' She regarded Paul solemnly and laughed. 'Look after her,' she said and he couldn't decide if she meant Eileen or Emma.

'Ever felt unwanted?' The car was on the ferry and they looked back at the Island which by now was bathed in sunlight as if the storm last night had never been, but the Solent was choppy and the ferry rolled as it left harbour.

'You know that's not true but knowing Emily and being a fervent convert to her powers, we may find Eileen already in labour when we get home.'

'No, Paul. If that was true my aunt would have turned us away from the door unfed and unrested!'

'Are you all right?'

'Cold and a bit queasy. They didn't flatten the sea for us and I hate rolling troughs.'

'I thought that you were never seasick.'

'Not often. I can stand really rough weather, but this wallowing does make me uneasy.'

'We'll soon be there. I see the jetty so it will be only five more minutes.'

'Let's stop for a few minutes after we dock,' Emma suggested.

Paul drove to a side road overlooking the car ferry port and they sat with the windows down so that Emma could recover. She took deep breaths and her colour returned. 'I'm fine now. Let's get home.'

'If you are sure, but I can stop on the way if you need a break from the car.'

The drive to London was uneventful and Emma forgot that she'd felt sick. Paul seemed anxious to get home too and when they arrived at the house, the peace and silence was an anticlimax.

Paul rang Mick's apartment to say that he was back and to enquire about Eileen.

'Get the push did you Doc? Eileen is a bit breathless but not as much as she was. Her waterworks give her no peace. She's in the lav every ten minutes as the baby is pressing on her bladder, the nurse said. Can't even go to the shops.'

'Tell her to rest. I think that means the baby is coming down and she may be in labour soon.'

'The hospital know about her but do you think I ought to ring them?'

'No, Mick. Wait until she's in labour. They wouldn't thank you for telling them she has frequency! It may take days to bring the baby into a birth position.'

'She says he's struggling to get out all the time! It can't be a girl. He kicks as hard as a professional footballer,' he added with pride.

'You haven't watched many girls playing hockey. They can be vicious.'

Emma laughed at her husband's comment, then went to her room. Eileen had attended the clinic regularly, first every month then every week and she was due for a checkup tomorrow. At least she thought it must be tomorrow, but time had fled, with Dwight's visit and the trip to the Island. Emma had lost count of the days. She picked up her diary and leafed through the notes. There was a mention of Eileen's next appointment and the expected date of her delivery. An asterisk at regular intervals showed that Emma's periods came each month like clockwork but either she'd forgotten to make a note of the last one, or she'd missed one.

Her mouth was dry and she sank down onto the bed. It couldn't be! She looked at her reflection in the mirror on the dressing table. Pale but certainly no longer ill after the flu. Perhaps fever of any kind could upset the hormones and she would find that this was a false alarm. *False?* Oh God, let it be true.

'Tea's made,' Eileen called. 'I'll take it into the office and we can all have some.'

Slowly, Emma went into the office and sat down by the desk where Eileen had placed her cup. She sipped the tea and made a wry face.

'What's wrong? I made it fresh but I left it to you to add sugar. Sometimes you do and sometimes you don't,' Eileen reminded her.

Emma had a vision of Emily's face,

her dark eyes triumphant. She took a dry biscuit, and looked at Paul who was smiling. 'You knew!' she accused him. 'You and Emily and I'm the last to know.'

Eileen had gone to fetch more hot water and to tell Mick that there was tea and biscuits waiting.

'I did wonder when my wife abandoned herself to me with great enthusiasm at a time when I thought she would be unavailable.' He grinned. 'It was good!'

'You sly beast! You and Aunt Emily! I wondered what you two were talking about when I was making parsley sauce.' Emma's eyes began to sparkle. 'You really think it could be ... that?' The smile faded. 'I don't think I could bear it if it isn't true. We can't be sure, can we? Not yet?'

'I'll drive Eileen in tomorrow and then take you over to Beatties for tests. I made an appointment from the Island and Stella will be ready for you before she starts her surgery.' Paul kissed her. 'Try not to say anything to the others until we are sure.'

'You seem sure.'

'We'll have the official diagnosis tomorrow, but as soon as Emily said you had a certain pallor about you and a pinched look about your nose, I didn't need an obstetrician to tell me what was happening.'

'She's too good to burn as a witch, but it's a bit unnerving. No tea for a while, but I don't fancy sour lemons like Sophie did.' She tipped away the tea in the sink of the clinical room and sat quietly when Eileen and Mick came into the room.

'I'll drive Eileen in tomorrow and then go on to Beatties. I have to see someone and Emma can meet an old friend. Wait for us to collect you, Eileen, and we can stop off and do any shopping we need, on the way home.'

## Chapter Thirteen

'I'd like you to take Eileen in this morning. I'm tied up just now and I'll go in to Beatties when you come back.'

'OK, Doc. I did want to see the nurse before Eileen is admitted to see if she has another list of things to take in. Eileen lost the first list, and didn't like to ask for another one, silly girl.'

'It's wise to know what they need, but when she's admitted she will wear a hospital gown at first until it's all over and then she may be able to wear her own nighties.' Paul went into the bedroom where Emma lay on the bed, white-faced and trembling.

This is ridiculous, he thought. I was talking about Eileen's list of clothes as if that was the most important thing on my mind! I never believed I could feel so weak-minded.

'I need a psychiatrist,' he said and was pleased to see that Emma found it amusing.

'It's good to know you care,' she said and rushed for the bathroom, leaving him feeling helpless, as if he'd never before seen a sick woman.

'Better now?' he asked hopefully.

'I'm sure I've finished. I'm hungry.'

'Do I cancel the appointment?'

'No, I shall eat some dry toast and and have a cup of Bovril and get dressed. It worked when I was seasick as a child and I think it's what I need now.'

'Well, take a bowl in the car just in case,' Paul remarked, but noticed that Emma's colour was returning fast.

She dressed and went down to the office to check notes until Mick brought Eileen back in the car. Emma was tempted to ask her when she had stopped having morning sickness but drew back. She was now quite sure that she was pregnant but she wanted to have the official verdict before telling anyone besides Paul—except that he knew before I did, she thought with amused resentment. She promised herself a phonecall to Aunt Emily later in the day.

Everything had a glow, an extra bloom as she straightened the cushions in the waiting room and smelled the flowers in the deep, wide bowl on the hall table. The sun showed up bright patches on the coloured glass in the front porch, making the door seem encrusted with emeralds and rubies.

'Won the pools?' Mrs Coster looked at her curiously.

'No, it's just a nice day.'

'Never heard you singing before. You should join the choral.' Mrs Coster leaned back on her heels in the middle of her scrubbed hall and regarded Emma with interest. 'You always look better after you've been down to see your auntie. If I didn't know better, with the doc being such a lovely man, I'd say you had another fella!' She laughed uproariously. 'Don't say I said that.'

'I should think not.' But Emma's mouth twitched and she laughed with a joy that threatened to burst out.

'Ready?' Paul had a carrier bag in his hand and handed it to Emma. 'We'll have something to eat after I've been to Beatties,' he said and added softly, so that Mrs Coster couldn't hear, 'that is, if you feel like eating anything but coal or caviar and don't have to use this.'

There was a new radiance between them and Emma realised that she had not been the only one to be acutely disappointed that they'd not as yet made a baby.

'Thanks,' she said dryly when they were in the car and she peeped into the carrier bag. 'You give me the most wonderful presents, Darling.' She lifted out the large pudding basin and the small towels. 'I knew these awful towels must be for something. They are too small for hand towels and the embroidery, done by one of your besotted patients for you to use in the consulting room, is very scratchy, so they are too rough for taking off make-up, and I could find no use for them if I couldn't use them for that; but for sicky women I suppose they are fine!'

'I thought the pudding basin would seem less obvious than a metal dish from the steriliser,' Paul announced with pride.

'If I am sick nobody would notice what the dish was like,' she replied with an ominous frown.

'You don't feel ...'

'Keep your eyes on the road. No, of course I'm fine. I'm over it for the day. Unlike Bea, I have no intention of being ill at any other time.'

'I'm glad we came home when we did. Another day and you might have been really ill on the ferry.'

'Not the same,' she replied with the newly acquired wisdom of someone who had never before felt like she had that morning.

Even the weathered stones of the old hospital glowed with light and the flower beds by the car park seemed more colourful than usual. 'Everything I see is enhanced,' she whispered. 'You didn't give me a hallucinogenic drug in my Bovril did you?'

'So that's why I feel as you do. It must have been Mrs Coster,' he agreed.

'I thought that even she looked ... quite reasonable this morning, but I'll stand by you now that you are pregnant.'

'Great! I have every intention of being unbearable at times. I've watched Bea and Eileen and I know just what to do to get my own way.'

'I shall beat you,' he said with delight. 'Oh, Emma I am so happy. Come on, let's see the lady and be told what we already know.'

The hospital smell was familiar and yet alien now that Emma came as a patient to her own training school. They waited for five minutes and then Stella Morgan came out of her consulting room, beaming. 'Paul seems to think you are pregnant.'

'After this morning, I am sure,' Emma said with feeling. She followed Stella into the room and was examined.

'Early yet, but definite. You have enough room in your pelvis to have a good delivery, your blood pressure is fine and you are not anaemic.' Stella watched Emma dress and smiled. 'Shaking the tree seems to have worked and I'm almost as thrilled as you are. Emma Sykes, you are going to have a baby and you can now tell everyone and bore them to death!'

'It's wonderful. I can't thank you enough, Stella.'

The consultant laughed. 'Paul did have something to do with it! Never forget that. Some women do.'

'He's as happy as I am.'

'I could see that. Now then, how is Bea and the twins. I heard a rumour that she is having another.'

'That's right.' Emma laughed. 'I hadn't thought of it but the babies will be born within a month of each other.'

'I shall expect to see them when she brings them back here. Come to see me next month for a checkup; bring a specimen and start antenatal exercises after the three months is up.' She opened the door and Emma hurried away to tell Paul.

'I can spare another couple of hours but it's too early for lunch. If you're hungry we could have something in a café,' he suggested.

'I am starving.' Emma peered out of the window. 'It's still there!'

Paul slowed the car. 'What do you see that I don't?'

'That café on the corner. Park over there and we'll go in.'

'It looks terrible. Do I have to bend to the woman's every crazy whim?' He sighed and parked the car outside the church next door to the café. 'With any luck if anyone I know spots the car they'll think we are in church.'

'Don't you dare to find fault with what was our lifeline when I was training and food was scarce.'

'You ate here?'

'After night duty we were all famished and the food was awful. Who wants breakfast at night and warmed up dinner in the morning? Not much of it and very unappetising most of the time.'

She pushed on the grimy glass door and Paul followed her with less enthusiasm. 'So this is London, glamorous capital city of England!'

'They still have the lift-up compartments for hot plates,' she discovered with glee. 'I hope they have my favourite.'

'I'll have coffee and a Danish pastry if it's not stale.'

'Coward!' Emma lifted a metal flap and drew out a steaming dish. 'This saved my life more than once. We decided that this was the most filling and delicious thing they served, and we'd done our research

250

by trying every dish in turn.'

Paul watched her with amused disbelief. 'Suet pudding with golden syrup?'

'Haven't you ever eaten in an ABC café?'

'I didn't train in London,' he reminded her. 'We had Cadena cafés and British Restaurants and a very suspect blackmarket café where they served huge pieces of fish with chips, and sometimes if we went early in the evening, real steak that wasn't whale meat. Probably horse but really edible. They had under-the-counter whiskey of uncertain origin, supposedly Irish.'

'I think I know which one. Bea and I went there before we came to London.' She paused with the full spoon halfway to her mouth.'

'Gone off the idea of stodge?'

'Not at all.' She resumed eating but looked thoughtful and her eyes held distant images. 'We were there one night in the Blitz. That was the night when our best friend and her brother were killed. Sadness blurs round the edges in time but I still think of her, and so does Bea.'

'That looks surprisingly good. I wish I was hungry enough to have that.'

'It's wonderful. I shall come here each

251

time I have a checkup with Stella. I doubt if anyone will try to pick me up in my condition.'

'Did they then?' Paul was amused.

'Bea and I were here and a spivvy-looking man came over and sat with us. He had a weird chat-up line. He said he'd seen us the night before on stage at the local music hall and he'd been very impressed. When we said it was a case of mistaken identity, he wanted to know what we did and where we lived, but Bea soon sent him off, saying we were waiting for our policemen boyfriends.' She laughed. 'Out of curiosity we looked at the pictures outside the music hall and decided we had been the two girls in grass skirts and we weren't flattered.'

'What a full life you lived.'

'Fuller now.' Emma patted her stomach. 'I don't think I'll have another pud today but your Danish pastry doesn't look at all bad. Do you want it all?'

Wordlessly, with a kind of admiration he pushed his plate across to her and watched her eat it with relish.

'They say it's an old wives' tale that pregnant women should eat for two but I think the old wives were right.'

'You'll grow fat, you'll eat us out of house and home and we'll end up bankrupt.'

'Glory be!'

'Mrs Sykes, we have things to do.'

'Yes, Sir.' But her eyes were still full of dreams. 'I must ask Eileen about her antenatal. There was no time to talk when she came back and I suppose it might happen at any time now.'

Paul closed the car door carefully, as if the vehicle was loaded with eggs, and went round to the driver's side. 'You mustn't do too much now. If Eileen needs help we ought to get a girl in to do the rougher house jobs. They say that pregnant women should do as much as possible sitting down and you must have a bed rest in the afternoons.'

'Let's get this clear, Paul. I am not ill and Stella stressed that I must lead a normal life, so after the first three months, during which time I shall not lift heavy articles or run a mile over hurdles, I shall be better if I exercise regularly and eat sensibly, but I say again, I am not ill.'

He drove slowly back to the house. 'It's just that everything now seems doubly precious. I thought we had everything I could desire but this is different. Now I know that the pregnant fathers I've met aren't going round the bend. They are just anxious and happy. I apologise to Dwight for laughing when he was over the moon about the twins.'

'He was a bit dramatic,' she agreed. 'I must telephone Washington with our world-shattering news.'

'We must time the call right. If you ring when they have early morning over there, you might be unlucky and get Bea in mid-puke!'

'It would be wonderful if she was here and we could go through this together.'

'Heaven forbid! You can write long letters to her when you are having your afternoon rest. Suddenly I am surrounded by fertility and I am out of my depth. I want to get back to my nice peaceful consulting room and the routine of my psychotic patients!'

'Stop here and I can do the shopping. Yes!' she told him when he demurred. 'Eileen will not be able to do it as she spends half her time in the lav and I shall pick up heavy things in the car in future unless Mick is available. We need potatoes, so you can help with them, and

I'll ask them to deliver a sack of King Edwards and a smaller sack of carrots. I think I shall eat lots of vegetables now and I need a huge pot of Bovril and some cocoa if I'm off tea.'

'I hope we have proper meals.' Paul pretended to be scared. 'I can't exist on boiled potatoes and Bovril.'

'I shall have extra rations, like Eileen. I hope I like milk now and I'll buy cod liver oil capsules as I doubt if I could stomach the oil they give in the clinics.'

'You are becoming very bossy,' he told her with affection.

'I know. There will be so much to plan for and I feel wonderful.'

Mrs Coster had finished for the morning, to Emma's relief, as she knew that for a while they could avoid her tales of death in childbirth and deformed babies, born to women who didn't do as they should in pregnancy, but giving no details of what was the correct method of carrying an unborn baby. She was fascinated by all aspects of the dangers of birth and the fact that she had so many healthy children didn't seem to have any bearing on what she thought of as grim reality. Eileen had refused to talk to her on many occasions.

Emma got through on the house phone and spoke to Mick. 'Everything all right?'

'Not long now. They said the head is down and she could be in labour at any time. You know what Eileen is. She worries that you will have too much to do when she's in hospital and nothing I say will convince her that you won't be overworked.'

'I'll pop down later, Mick. Tell her that in future we'll have groceries and vegetables delivered to save time and I have other labour-saving plans in mind.' Her lips twitched. Literally labour-saving but that was in the distant future and Eileen had enough on her mind at present. The good news would have to wait.

After lunch, Emma felt too stimulated to rest. She walked about, arranging and rearranging cushions and newspapers until Paul told her bluntly that she must relax. 'Get on with the notes if you need an occupation, and ring your aunt as soon as she comes back from Dr Sutton's surgery.'

Mick appeared in the office doorway. 'I didn't want her to hear me use the blower, but can you spare a minute, Sister?'

Eileen was perspiring. 'I had a pain but

it wasn't too bad. Give me your watch, Mick. I have to time them, the nurse said.' She forced a smile. 'Packed my case.'

'Very wise. I have nothing to do this afternoon so I'll sit here for a while if you like.' Mick nodded gratefully and Emma was amused that such a strong man could look so plaintive, as if he was the one in labour!

'Do you think I should ring the hospital?'

'Not yet. Unless the membranes burst, Eileen has a long way to go.' Emma picked up Eileen's wrist and took her pulse. 'Fine,' she said, cheerfully. 'Since we had the flu, I made a few decisions. In normal times neither of us is overworked but we shall have a baby in the house and when Bea was here we all had a lot to do. I shall ask Mrs Coster to work for an extra day a week and take over the rest of the heavy work in future as she has already hinted more than once that she could spare the time. I'd like a little more time for my own friends.' She smiled. 'It sounds self-indulgent but we all need a break and when you come home I want to share your baby as I did with Bea.'

'I thought I was letting you down.'

'Rubbish.' Emma spoke briskly. She wanted to tell them about the baby but held back. This was Eileen's party!

They timed the contractions and Mick made coffee, hovering anxiously until Paul asked him to join him in the office. 'I might as well do some work if Sister's there.'

Eileen sighed and winced again, then sat back in the big chair. It was hot and the sky was dark through the open window. 'If only the heat would break, I'd be more comfortable. Being in bed for a few days doesn't bear thinking about.'

'A pity you can't have it in the cool at Christmas like ... Bea.' Emma bit her lip. Whoops, I nearly said it. This was no time to expect Eileen to have an ecstatic reaction to the news of another woman's pregnancy.

As the long bright rays of afternoon sun mellowed Eileen gasped and Emma made sure that the couch on which she now lay was covered with newspapers and towels. Emma dialled the number of the hospital and asked for an ambulance and then called for Mick.

'Her waters have broken,' she said simply. 'An ambulance will be better and

258

safer than taking her in the car.'

Mick gathered up the case and his own coat and umbrella as the rain wasn't far away and he'd have to come home by bus. He hurried away and Paul and Emma subsided into deep armchairs as soon as the ambulance had gone.

'Will it be like this?' Paul sounded apprehensive.

'Not for six or seven more months.'

'You didn't tell them? If you had, Mick would have mentioned it.'

'When I am like that I want everyone to think of *me* and Eileen must have her baby before we tell them. It's only fair.'

'You amaze me. I nearly told Mick and you must have been eager for her to know.'

'As Aunt Emily said ... there's a time for everything and anything good is worth waiting for.'

'Ring her now, before she rings you and tells you the exact date of your baby being born!'

'I'll ask her for the small cot that she had there for Clive when he was tiny. It saved Aunt Janey and George having to bring one with them when they came to stay.'

'If I know her, she'll have the wickerwork

259

dusted and fixed up with a new mattress before you ask.'

Before Emma could lift the receiver, the phone rang.

'Dr Sykes' residence.'

'Is that you, Emma?'

'Aunt Emily! What a nice surprise.' Paul shook his head and laughed at Emma's innocent expression.

'How are things?' Emily sounded excited.

'You mean Eileen? She's in labour and went to the hospital half an hour ago. She's fine.'

'Not Eileen. What about you?'

'I'm fine too,' Emma giggled. 'All right, it's cruel to tease you. Yes I am and yes I've seen the obstetrician to confirm that Emma Sykes is going to have a baby.'

'Holy Mary! It surely is true at last.' Emily sounded very Irish and used the expression that nobody in the family had heard for years, one that her mother, Jane Darwen had used in moments of stress or joy. 'I have the small cot ready. You can collect it when you come down again or I'll send it by carrier.'

'Paul said you might have it ready.'

'Cheeky thing! Give him my love.'

# Chapter Fourteen

Mrs Coster looked on with evident disapproval. 'Fed all mine.'

Emma eyed the woman's large pendulous breasts, bulky under her tight blue blouse as if trying to escape. 'Some are luckier than others,' she replied tactfully. 'Eileen just didn't produce enough to satisfy a hungry baby so the sister in postnatal put the baby on the bottle.'

'I must say it's convenient,' Mrs Coster admitted reluctantly. 'Eileen does like to get out and do the shopping and you don't seem to mind helping out so I suppose it's as well to get some practice before you have your own.' As usual, Mrs Coster looked at her employer as if she couldn't believe that she was pregnant. 'Not showing much yet, are you?'

'It's early. I'm only just over the first few months and I can still get into my clothes.'

It was late August 1949 and Mick and Eileen were shopping for supplies, as

Dwight and Bea were coming to stay while Dwight attended an important meeting at the Foreign Office in Whitehall.

'Did Dwight get through? Do they need us to pick them up?' Paul hovered in the kitchen doorway and watched his wife de-wind baby Jean before putting her in the light wicker Moses basket that could be carried from room to room with ease.

'As usual, Dwight has organised everything. They have an official car and a driver while they are here and as they left the twins in America, they can concentrate on his duties.' Emma looked serious. 'The fact that they could bear to leave the twins means that this visit is of great importance and not a family holiday.'

'I've heard rumours. One of my patients is at last getting over battle fatigue. He is out of the services but he has two brothers, one in the Navy and one in the army so he hears a lot of semi-secret news. He mentioned a lot of rows between heads of state and a fear that General MacArthur might do something rash. He's a brilliant soldier but is full of his own importance.'

'Surely he has to obey Washington. He can't do exactly as he wishes.'

'He's in Japan and far from Washington.

He is fond of misconstruing orders when it suits him and he is building up a great reputation over there as the Japs feel that through him they will find their freedom again and the face they lost in defeat. Although they aren't allowed to build arms—that is in theory—they are now doing so. MacArthur has opened factories and given permission for them to get back into production to provide weapons for Korea, so ironically, the man who once accepted their surrender is now considered something of a deliverer.'

'I'll take the baby down to Eileen to change and dress. I heard them come in and Bea will want to see her as soon as she arrives. She may think the baby very small after being with her fast-growing twins. It's a shame that they couldn't come too but thank Heaven for Bea's visit. I'm longing to see her.'

She gathered up the baby's paraphernalia and the cot to go down in the lift to the hall and then she walked on down to the basement flat.

'How's she been?' Eileen asked as if she had been far away from her baby for a week instead of a couple of hours. 'No, you mustn't pick her up, Mick. She has a tummyful and the last time you picked her up after a meal she was sick on your jacket.'

'She likes me to jiggle her up and down.'

'Later, after her sleep. I'm going to put her in that nice new smock with the embroidery, in case Mrs Bea arrives.'

Not only did the American driver bring them to the door but he carried their baggage up to the rooms that Bea and Dwight had used the last time they had lived in the house, and Bea and Emma trailed after Dwight, almost unable to speak, with emotion.

'Now what *don't* I offer you?' Emma asked with delight. 'I am off tea and anything too milky.'

'Tea, Yuck! Coffee so-so but Cocoa *yes*. Orange juice yes and lemons *no*. Isn't it just wunnerful that we are this-a-way together?'

'You look very smart, and not very pregnant.' Bea's light-grey swing-back jacket hid her waistline and the light-blue blouse made her eyes very blue.

'So do you, and you don't show at all. Maybe it's a false alarm.'

'Mrs Coster has her doubts about me,

but I assure you I am pregnant at last.'

Bea laughed when she saw the brass bedstead with the shining knobs. 'We sent the four-poster to Texas and have only slept in it for one week. Each month we thought we could go there to live, but Washington had other ideas and I'm lost without Dwight so I have to stay for a while longer.'

'It can't be bad.'

'I hate to say this but I love it. The wide open spaces no longer call me and I've met some good folk. Holiday times on the ranch will do for a while. We'll go there after the baby is born. Why should we suffer alone with broken nights when there will be a band of adoring women waiting to take a turn?'

'You haven't changed.'

'I hope not. I love my husband, I miss you and I'm dying to phone Aunt Emily.'

'You must see Eileen's baby first or she'll never forgive you.'

'You make them sound like family.'

'They are. Mick was marvellous when my mother died. He saw to everything and it's all wrapped up, the house has been sold and we have finished with lawyers and a horrible friend of my mother's and I need never go back there.'

'You needn't take any notice of me,' Dwight remarked in an offended voice, then picked up Emma and kissed her. 'My, my, how you have grown,' he said.

'Do that in six months' time and you'll say that,' Paul told him. 'I made coffee if that suits?'

'Fine,' Bea said. 'Not too strong and lots of sugar. We brought some with us in case you are still rationed.'

In the drawing room, Bea admired some prints that had not been there when she left England. 'What's this?' She stood below the newly framed picture, set where it could be seen easily and dominating the corner of the room.

'That's my grandmother; Aunt Emily's mother.'

'She's beautiful, but sad.'

'She had a hard life and seven children.'

'If I have seven children and look as good I shall be very pleased, but I hope I shall look happier than she does. What a gentle mouth. She must have been a good woman.'

'I believe she was.'

'Did you know her?'

'I think I met her when I was very small. I remember a woman with a long dark skirt and very gentle hands. Not soft hands, but worn and caring and smelling of apples. I've learned more about my family since my mother died than ever I knew when I was with her, as she seldom mentioned them.'

'Did Emily tell you?'

'She always answered any questions and I learned more when I met Uncle Sidney in America, but it was the letters and photographs and trinkets that brought them all to life. Aunt Emily was delighted to see them again as she thought that they were lost or destroyed. We had copies of all the photographs made for me and for George and she has the originals to give to Aunt Janey. Can't you imagine them sipping that terrible brew of tea and whisky and laughing and crying over the pictures?'

'I can't wait to see them. Don't forget, I consider them to be my family too!' Bea looked mischievous. 'What did cousin George think about you having a baby.'

'Pleased, I think, but Aunt Emily doesn't encourage us to meet or to communicate very often. If he married again, and I think there is a Wren he sees now, we might get

267

together with the children. Clive might like to play with his cousin later.' She thought for moment.

'What would be a cousin's child to me? A second cousin or a cousin once removed? I never know.'

'What are you having? I'll have to get on the hotline to Emily and ask if she knows what Dwight and I are producing. Not twins again I hope, much as I love mine. I can't battle again with all those stretch marks. I did everything they told me about oiling my bulge and buttocks with olive oil but I didn't escape as I was huge at the end. The oil did make sex different,' she added complacently. 'I recommend it. Dwight said it was like making love to a slippery seal. I knew he liked swimming but I didn't know that he'd indulged in that sort of activity!' Emma clung to her as they dissolved into giggles.

'Talking about me?' Dwight asked as he brought in a tin of biscuits and some chocolate. 'I knew it was a mistake to let you two get together again. Just seen Eileen and the baby. It's cute. Were ours ever as small?'

'Why would we talk about you? Some men are so vain they think we can't talk of anything but them. We are discussing feminine things, babies and clothes.'

Bea looked angelic and he scowled happily. 'Christ! Let me out! I'm going to bed. I have to face a lot of iron men tomorrow and try to keep the peace, and my fatigue is showing.' He smiled tenderly. 'You should rest too, Honey. That bed looks great and I'll crash out as soon as I hit the sack.' He yawned. 'Wake me up when it's time for food. Eileen wants to see you and show off what she produced.' Dwight was suddenly serious. 'They may ask why we came just now. Say anything but never mention my job. It's top secret and anything we say here must go no further but I have to talk to someone I can trust or go mad. Thank God you are here.'

Paul reassured him. 'I've told them that it wouldn't be safe for Bea to fly after six months and she wanted to see Emma before they have their babies. You are also visiting friends in the services and seeing your godfather and Bea's family who feel neglected.'

'Want to tag along tomorrow? You might just prevent a third world war. Thanks Paul.'

'Do you have to go to Korea?' Emma was worried.

'Not to fight.' He spoke quickly. 'The naval and marine commanders have gathered in Dai Inchi Mal with a lot of top brass from Washington to discuss the future in Korea. Some say it's an impossible mission to invade the North, some want to bulldoze in at any cost and the United Nations want to be a simple peacekeeping force.'

'So why is there a meeting in London?'

'Discussions,' Dwight shrugged. 'Then we go quietly over to South Korea and see MacArthur and his fire-eater cohorts and we hope to be able to put him straight if we know a few facts and can show a concerted front. If the experts say that an invasion would be possible from the sea at Inchon, so be it, but it's very tricky. Radford, Sherman and Collins have to be consulted, but first we need a lot of information about the local territory.'

'Get some sleep.' Bea kissed him and gently propelled him towards the door. 'We can all talk later.'

'Right, Honey.' They heard him close the bedroom door and Bea went down to see the new baby, trying to seem as if there would be no war, and no bloodshed or widows and bereaved parents left to mourn another new set of young dead.

'She's beautiful,' Bea said with enthusiasm. 'What a pretty smock.'

Eileen was triumphant. Mick had said that Bea wouldn't notice the new garment but she had! At last Emma stopped Eileen's flow of words and firmly told Bea to have a rest. They walked up to the bedrooms. 'She was delighted that you noticed that rather awful new smock,' she said.

'Did I?' Bea grinned. 'When I went to Washington, I was asked to talk about England at war and to judge a few baby beauty contests. One of the wives who had done that stint for years took me aside. "You don't say anything really useful or truthful when you judge a show. You pick the baby with the most belligerent-looking mother to avoid repercussions when it's over and as they all have new clothes for a shindig like that you can say to everyone how nice they look, even if it kills you. You also say that you have never seen such a wunnerful selection of babies and you love them all!" It works a treat and as yet I haven't been lynched.'

'Eileen was delighted.'

'They all are,' Bea replied easily. 'Not the prettiest baby I've seen, but healthy, and the jewel in Mick's crown, so why compare her to my beautiful twins?'

Emma chuckled. 'I bet you've never put them into a beauty parade.'

'I should think not. Have them exposed to all those coughs and colds and a stupid woman judge who wouldn't know a perfect baby from a monkey?'

'You could always look stroppy and menacing, then you'd be sure to win.'

'That's what I miss about you, Dewar. You have no respect for me and it's wonderful.'

'You are improving. When you arrived, everything was so American and wunnerful, and now you said wonderful as you did when you lived here.'

'It does rub off.' Bea was apologetic. 'I try to fly the flag and they just *love* my accent but would you believe that I said, "Have a nice day" last week? I'd vowed never to use that expression but it slipped out.'

'What do you want to eat tonight? I'll get it ready while you have a nap.'

'Would you mind?' Bea looked shame-faced.

'You must eat something and Dwight will be ravenous, unless he's changed a lot.'

'We talked on the plane and agreed that there was one very special dish we craved.'

'Both of you? I thought you had come from the land of the fleshpots. Dwight has no right to be faddy. He isn't pregnant.'

'Fish and chips. They don't do that well over there. Lobster Thermidor yes, Grilled prawns or smoked salmon, yes, but good old British fish and chips, no! They haven't got the hang of crisp batter that tastes of something other than flour or chips cooked in beef dripping.'

Emma laughed. 'That's easy, and I'll make a salad. We have a lot of fresh fruit and some cheese so even Dwight will have enough.'

'See you later after our rests.'

'I'll tell Paul when to wake me and we can eat at leisure.' She went to find Paul.

'It all sounds quiet.' Paul took his attention from the appointment book. 'Is there much to do? Tell me how I can help.'

'You can fetch the fish and chips later,

and toss the salad if you're good. Don't look so surprised. Special request for tonight and you know Dwight loves it. Bea and I can have snacks tomorrow when Dwight is at the Foreign Office and you are at St Thomas's.'

'Will you be here all day?'

'Probably not. I can leave the office to Mick as you have no appointments booked for tomorrow and he knows by now what to accept and not to promise anything that he knows you would refuse, like the patient who needed to be in a safe hospital but his GP tried to persuade you to take him in here as a resident patient.'

'That was impossible, and Dr Morgan knows better than to try it again. He said he had ordered an ambulance to bring the man here, assuming that once he arrived here we would have to admit him. He was very high-handed, as if he had that right.'

'What happened? I was ill at that time and never knew the details.'

'It was no use arguing and telling him that we are not a registered nursing home, so I rang Benson at the psychiatric unit and said a patient would be on his way there for investigation. I waited outside for the ambulance; I said there had been a mistake and Benson's team was expecting the patient as I didn't take in-patients here under any circumstances. I re-routed the ambulance. The GP was annoyed as the family were influential and wealthy and wanted a private place for him, preferably as an only patient.'

'I can see the problem but it was naughty of the doctor to try it on with you. I remember a phonecall from a GP asking us to admit a kidney patient into our acute surgical ward which wasn't geared for chronic long-stay cases. We had enough to do to cope with very ill patients who needed genito-urinary surgery.'

Paul nodded sympathetically. 'It wasn't acute but the doctor wanted the case off his hands?'

'How did you guess? The admitting clerk asked for details of his condition and was told that he needed urgent investigation, but when he was admitted it was evident that he had been chronically sick for weeks and was in the last stages of kidney failure. He was in a coma. It was bad and quite wrong for that ward so he had to go to the geriatric ward where he died two days later.'

Paul hugged her and smiled ruefully. 'Rest now and think beautiful thoughts, Darling. Strange people, aren't we? Even in our happiest moments we can never forget our work, our calling. Forget the hassle of all that and look forward.'

'I do, and now that I can be objective, it doesn't worry me at all. In fact, it makes me realise just how happy I am.'

'Good! Just don't reminisce with Bea too much. I think Dwight and I can do without you weeping over your fish and chips.'

'As if we would.'

He grinned. 'Then who were Dwight and I sitting with in church one Christmas Eve, when two pretty girls drenched our handkerchiefs with their memories of the war?'

Emma tried to appear dignified. 'You as a psychiatrist should know that tears are cathartic and very useful.'

'Yes, Ma'am. Go and rest!'

Emma picked up the photograph album to browse through in bed but after two minutes it slipped from her fingers and she slept, stirring an hour later with a feeling of great contentment and wondering why she felt as she did, then remembered that Bea and Dwight were in the same house and had brought that mood with them.

She showered and dressed and tiptoed past the room where her visitors slept soundly. Would the Victorians who had slept in that bed think the present occupants an incongruous couple under the crimson damask coverlet, with the brass knobs of the bedstead gleaming softly and the faded Victoriana of the room giving the lie to the expensive American garments scattered over the chairs?

'I left him to sleep,' Bea said an hour later when she reappeared, yawning. 'I'm thirsty.' She examined the bottles on the kitchen shelf. 'Oh, goody! Real concentrated National Health orange juice for mothers and babies. I'd forgotten it was so good. I drank it by the gallon when I was here expecting the twins and I bought the rations of it from a couple of girls in antenatal who hated it.'

'If they were undernourished, they might have needed it.'

'One admitted that she tipped one lot down the sink at home so that she could take the bottle back as requested and the other one had never drunk orange squash let alone the proper stuff and wouldn't take it, so I wasn't depriving them of anything.

As I payed them for it very generously they had a little extra to spend on what they really liked. One had a passion for Tizer, if I remember rightly.'

'As it's free, they should have tried to drink it. Usually women enjoy it. They should take and use their rations.'

Bea laughed, 'OK Sister Sykes. Tell me, how much of that ghastly cod liver oil do you drink?'

Emma blushed. 'All right, I am as bad. I was sick when I tried to force some down and I buy capsules now.' She laughed. 'However, the neighbour has three cats who now have very smooth, gleaming fur and walk around giving off an aura of fish oil. Mrs Coster shoos them away whenever she smells them coming.'

'The twins have a kitten each now as they can't ride and they needed a pet to teach them some manners. They have learned that *no* means don't tease. The kittens never try to reason with them as Dr Spock would have us do—they just scratch! The twins are learning fast and they really don't treat them badly. The silly pusses like them.'

'We have time to look at the album

before supper when the men take over.' They sat on the deep settee and Bea asked questions and remarked on the faces she saw. From time to time they gazed at the picture of Jane Darwen, the woman who had founded Emma's family and Bea was entranced by her. 'I wish she was mine. My grandmothers were terrible. Neither of them loved me and they spent their time on the Riviera and then Switzerland during the wars. No wonder my mother was shallow and vain and couldn't get me off her hands quickly enough.'

'You have a good father.'

'He mellowed,' Bea admitted. 'I must get in touch and see him before we go back, although he did come to us last month on business. Miranda has worked on him and I found him quite civilised. No little weekend popsies now. He hovers over her and makes her keep to her diabetic diet and rest whenever she can leave the stage. They are really happy.'

'Aren't we all?'

'Sure thing. It's a miracle.' A noise on the floor above alerted Bea. 'I hear Dwight crashing about looking for his socks or something. We could be ready for our feast soon!'

279

# Chapter Fifteen

'Do you want to go to Beatties?'

Bea looked uncertain and sighed. 'No, I don't want to discuss my pregnancy, as I have my own gynae team back home and I doubt if I know many people who we knew in our day.' She laughed softly. 'In our day! That sounds so ancient.'

'I know how you feel. I go there to see Stella and I hope to have the baby there, but it's true that we have left for good and that life goes on and changes all the time. We can't live in the past, even if we learned a lot on the way.'

'Remember Nurse Warren?' Bea smiled wryly. 'A lesson to us all.'

'Warren?'

'The girl who adored Beatties so much that when she left to work in paediatrics at Great Ormond Street, she came back every week on her day off to see us all. She wanted to be sister of the children's ward if it became vacant, but honestly, she was a pain and got in the way of our work, and there was never anyone off duty who really welcomed her as they'd made their own arrangements. In time everyone tried to avoid her. You must remember her.'

'I do now you mention her. I felt sorry for her. She had no time to make friends at GOSH as she dashed off in her spare time to see us and then found she had little in common as our staff was changing all the time and she had no place in what we were doing any more.'

'Fell between two stools, as I've heard Aunt Emily say.'

'We aren't like that.'

'Thank God for that, but I see the danger in looking back too often. We are true friends Emma, and will be even more so in the future as our children grow up, but we have two separate lives now and we are happy in our marriages.' Bea shook her blonde head. 'It isn't fair! We should have been sisters.'

'I've thought that so many times, but you would have been my sister by choice, not just because we were from the same family. Emily didn't feel kinship with two of her sisters and she's lost touch with one brother. She loved the one who died in America and she is close to Janey. Families are strange and blood relationships don't always work out.'

'God gave us our relations but allowed us to make our own friends!' Bea laughed. 'We are becoming very profound but it's all true.'

'When do you go back?'

'You sound like people at home during the war. Mick said that it drove the men bananas to be asked that even before they'd put their kitbags inside the door—"When are you going back?"—as if they weren't wanted.'

'Silly! I want to know what we can fit in. Is there time to visit Emily?'

'Not on this occasion. I have to be ready to leave at a moment's notice if Dwight has to report back to Washington, but if he goes to Korea, I might stay on for a few days.' Bea pushed back her hair with an impatient gesture. 'What am I saying? I miss my lovely, naughty twins and yet I want to stay here. This was home and England holds so much of my life that is precious, but now I know that I shall follow Dwight wherever he wants to be and where his duties take him. I'm like Ruth in the Bible. I go where he goes and his people shall be my people. The US of

282

A isn't bad Emma. Why don't you come over? Paul could make a fortune as they are crying out for men like him and we would have a marvellous time.' Her pleading was almost frightening.

Emma smiled sadly. 'We'll come over for a holiday sometime when Paul decides to take up the offer of a lecture tour, but I've only recently discovered some of my roots and I am tied here.' She looked up at the picture of Jane Darwen. 'I want to find out more about her. Each time I look at that picture, I see the real woman and I wish I'd known her.'

Bea's voice shook. 'Why do you think I want you over there with me? I am jealous. I wish I'd had two lovely aunts and a grandmother like that. You say you didn't know her. Look in the mirror when you feel sad and she'll stare back at you.'

'You share the aunts,' Emma said defensively. 'You spent long enough on the phone to Aunt Emily last night!'

Bea chuckled. 'For someone who swears she doesn't really like children, she is amazing! I had to tell her every detail about the twins and I sensed that she would love to come over and visit but she says she can't. And is she thrilled about

283

your news? She sure is.'

'She could visit America but it would take a lot of courage. It takes a major decision to go to see Aunt Janey in Hampshire! Besides, she is a busy lady and that can't be bad at her age. She's not one to sit around doing nothing for very long.'

'She ought to marry her nice doctor, but she dismisses the idea as ridiculous at her time of life.' Bea looked wicked. 'I made her admit that he had asked her several times, even though he is much younger than she is.'

'She had one lover and never found anyone to take his place, so she looked after her parents until they died, met her friends and made lovely crochet work instead.' Emma looked amused and put out a restraining hand, as if to ward off Bea's pleading. 'No, you can't have my lace bedspread so it's no use asking again. I shall wrap it up in blue tissue paper to prevent it going yellow and hand it down to my daughter.'

'You're sure you'll have a girl?'

'I don't know but that's what Emily thinks.'

'She wouldn't even guess at mine but

says I'll be fine and the baby healthy, so until something bad happens I'll believe her.'

'You wanted some snaps of London didn't you Bea? So let's go "Up West", as Mrs Coster says, and take a few of St James's Park and Trafalgar Square. Feeling fit for walking?'

'We can stop for lunch in a Lyons Corner House if there's one still standing.'

'A bit low key for you?'

'I know I didn't use them very often as Pa had his apartment in St James's but over there, back home, a lot of men who served in the war have nostalgic memories of the Nippies. I suspect they tried to pick up the pretty waitresses, as well as girls eating alone, when they believed they were safe from predatory men there in a respectable Jo Lyons. I shall feed their memories with pictures of girls with fluffy hair and black dresses and crisp white aprons and chequered head bands on their caps.'

'Don't forget their black stockings. They had the same effect on men as ours did. The admin at Beatties thought black stockings were dull and right for uniform and they never caught on to the fact that they made the otherwise healthy men in orthopaedics quite mad!'

'Even the lisle stockings had that effect and when nylons came in, wow!'

It was good to be together and to laugh at old times, to revive pleasant memories and firmly shut out the ones that hurt.

In Whitehall they looked up at the empty windows and wondered if Dwight was sitting in on one of the conferences, then they bought buns to give to the ducks in St James's Park and Bea swore she recognised one from way back. 'He recognised me, too.'

'Rubbish! Yours got caught by poachers last year when the park lost a lot and they ended up in cooking pots.'

'The twins will love this park. They must see it. We'll bring them over soon,' Bea promised.

'We have work to do first,' Emma reminded her gently.

'Work? Labour, you mean! Some day, we'll all come over, the twins and the new baby and Dwight and me, and stay for a long time.' Bea looked pale, as if she didn't really believe it could happen.

'We'll make it come true,' Emma assured her, but the time-gap was widening with the advent of the babies and Bea was now saying, "Back home" frequently. 'We may come to you first; who knows?'

'Time to go,' Bea announced after using up two rolls of film. 'I took some pictures of the ruined buildings covered with weeds and looking decidedly unsafe, as the Yanks think the war is over and that by now all signs of bomb damage have gone and we are back to normal, so it does them good to see what it's really like after all this time.'

'Why did you take so many?'

'It's odd but I was really interested. Coming back fresh to it all, I felt like a war correspondent. When I go back I shall get the pictures in some sort of order and tell the story of Britain after the war. I might even sell it to a magazine. It will be a good project to keep my mind off my tum and Korea.'

In the back of both their minds, Korea loomed large and Bea bought an *Evening Standard* to skim through and check that nothing new was reported. Dwight returned at seven, when they were wondering if he would have eaten and if he would be hungry. Paul took one look at him and rang the Italian

287

restaurant round the corner to order dinner.

'Let's eat first, Dwight. Take time to get your thoughts in order after today. After that we can discuss as much as you feel we can be told. A good meal will sort you out and we can talk when we are back here again in private.'

'This guy is so wise,' Dwight remarked as he drained his first glass of red wine. 'Being low on calories and having thoughts buzzing round my head made me feel unreal. I can see how a man staying in a hotel after a sticky conference must want to talk to someone, just anyone who listens, and he might give away important information.'

'During the war, posters reminded us of that. "Careless talk costs lives," was one and lonely soldiers must have been tempted to talk.'

'Pillow talk with pretty tarts?' Bea looked complacent. 'Why do you think I came all this way with my man?'

Dwight looked thoughtful and began to count on his fingers. 'Maybe I don't have to ring for a call girl. Could be OK now. I'll check tonight.'

They walked back in the soft warm night

and Dwight half-heartedly tossed a stone at two squalling alley cats.

'Missed. Remember Honey, you now like cats.'

'Only our kittens and they have lost at least six of their nine lives.'

Emma made coffee for the men and cocoa for her and Bea. Paul brought out a bottle of Grand Marnier and one of crème de menthe that Mrs Molten had insisted he must accept. He tried to believe they had not been bought on the black market.

Dwight was relaxed. He sighed and stretched his long legs on the big velvet-covered settee. 'More coffee,' he demanded and nobody suggested that it would keep him awake. 'It was a shambles,' he said at last. 'The brass hats who were back from Korea to brief the Brits and the French were divided about the situation. Some who had known Mac from way back, admired him as a forceful general but knew that he wanted fame and power above all else. They showed caution and a healthy cynicism and said he ought to cool it. The new boys were bowled over by his charisma and seemed to think he could work miracles.'

Paul regarded him solemnly. 'And you?

What is your opinion?'

'I've met him a couple of times and he does have a lot of glamour and an arrogance that defies anyone to say no to his plans, which if he's got it right is what is needed in a leader.'

'If he hasn't got it right, what then?'

'Loss of life, loss of equipment and what is important to any powerful nation, loss of face, with the whole world watching and American mothers gunning for him if he sacrifices their boys to a lost cause.'

'I know very little about Korea. If it wasn't that you were involved, we would treat it as a local difficulty on the other side of the world that has no place in our history.' Emma looked apprehensive.

Paul's mouth tightened. 'We're still picking up the pieces after the war and some of the pieces will never fit again, so as a nation we can't afford to take part in this one if it comes. We defend our own people and fight for a cause that we believe to be right but we'll dig in our heels if we are forced into a war outside our comprehension.'

Dwight nodded. 'It's all in the air and before they can do much more, there are lots of difficulties to overcome if the army is to invade North Korea effectively from the sea. Some say it can't be done but a few of the generals say it's possible to invade from Inchon, but they have to convince the Navy lords.'

'Why there?'

'For one thing it would take them by surprise because it's so unlikely as a terrain for landing. The tide there is one of the highest in the world with a range of over thirty-two feet. At low tide it's a quagmire that would bog down the landing craft but at high tide the boats could land easily and make a beachhead in a very advantageous position if they made it a fast operation with pretty slick organising.'

'I take it that you've studied the last war.'

'Sure. Everyone talked about the Anzio and other failed or expensive landings but others used the D-Day invasion of Normandy as their blueprint for an argument in favour of an invasion in difficult circumstances. The weather had to be considered for that one, the logistics were formidable and they had only a small window of opportunity, but they managed it, and here we are, ready to make more mistakes if we don't get our act together.'

'Would weather be a consideration?'

'The typhoon season would be on the way to bugger up the roads and transport, and if we leave it too long the monsoons will have arrived, so they have to make decisions fast. If they invade at high tide when they think it possible, they have only two hours of daylight left to bring equipment ashore and make it a safe facility.'

Paul watched Dwight's face. Almost casually he asked, 'What sort of cover would they have?'

Dwight sat up and drained his coffee cup and Bea looked anxious. 'Long range artillery from carriers and ... napalm from bombers.' He suddenly looked very tired. 'At least that what's been suggested and one moron even thought that a hydrogen bomb might be the answer to get it over quickly, but that was not a popular idea, thank God.'

'Was anything settled?'

'Not yet and not here in Whitehall, but the US navy are coming round to believe the invasion has possibilities. Rear Admiral James Doyle was cautious but said that Inchon was not impossible. He spoke as a sailor but the advance on land would be another matter with a few headaches for the army and air force.' He shrugged. 'I've finished here and they don't need me in Korea just now.'

'When do you want to go home, Darling?'

Dwight looked at his wife and smiled wearily. 'If you can drag yourself away, I guess any time they say I can leave—like the day after tomorrow?'

Bea's grip on the coffee pot tightened but her return smile was soft and reassuring. 'Any time, you say, Sir.'

'Is that OK?' He glanced anxiously at Emma.

'We have one whole day left?' She forced a laugh. 'Bea and I must shop for maternity clothes. I need her experience. Aunt Emily will have some made for me, but Bea will know what more I need, so no feeding ducks tomorrow, just hard work.'

'Bed now. We are all tired.' Paul put the used cups on the tray and carried them into the kitchen saying that Mrs Coster would see to them in the morning. He came back and kissed Bea on the cheek. 'Well done,' he whispered and she felt the heat of unshed tears under her eyelids. 'Fragile creatures, we men,' he added, grinned and turned away to Dwight who was looking for the shoes he'd discarded when he lay on the settee. 'Come on, Emma, I'm tired even if you aren't.' He saw her determined poise sagging and shooed her off to bed.

'You've just got to come to the States,' Dwight said with emotion. 'We need you.'

'Persuade Aunt Emily to let Emma go, first. Later, we'll visit you if we can hear ourselves talk over the chatter of all those children ... three of yours and one of ours,' he added with a certain satisfaction.

Dwight swayed, slightly drunk and ready for maudlin reflection. 'Tell you what, old Buddy. We'll have a boy, you have a girl and we'll betroth them when they are two.'

'Let's get them born first! They might both be girls and what if they hate each other on sight and pull each other's hair?'

'Come along, Genius,' Bea said and led Dwight to the brass bedstead and warmth and love. 'Junior is kicking and wants us to sleep.'

Emma was in bed but wide awake.

'Not upset that they are leaving?' Paul smoothed her hair and kissed her gently.

'Of course I am, but everything falls

into place now. We have to get on with having our babies and adapt to what that will bring. We know we are close all the time even if we don't see each other for months, even years. I know we can never grow away from each other, especially now that the barrier of my not having children has vanished. I know that it was a barrier of minor embarrassment even if we never admitted it. At times I shall feel bereft, Paul. I know I'll want to talk to her and see her reaction to what we have to say and to what we are doing here.'

'And she'll be the same. Bea has been very brave. From what Dwight told me, she was terribly homesick when they arrived in Washington but the babies helped and she made friends with other young mothers. Now, as usual, Bea is Queen Bee of several societies and in great demand to talk about "the Old Country". Her cut-glass British voice makes her very popular and Dwight says she charms all the crusty old veterans.'

'Now that the telephone service gives better quality communication I must use it more, and Bea wants to ring Aunt Emily sometimes direct so that she hears her news first-hand and not through me.'

'Do you mind sharing her?'

'No. Aunt Emily can talk about Bea to me after they've had their conversation and she'll love to tell Aunt Janey about it. It will make Bea closer to all of us, so she is welcome to share my family.'

'I'm glad they are leaving.'

'Paul!'

'Dwight needs to go back. He is on edge even if they have told him that he can go home and not go to talks in Korea.'

'Could he have a relapse?'

'Not very likely, but he may have that idea in the back of his mind. He does know what happened to him and dreads having to expose himself to any more military trauma, but it's something with which he must learn to cope on his own. I hope he manages to retire from the service completely. Annual dinners with old comrades and a few dressed-up appearances would suit him very well and they could leave Washington and live on the ranch.'

'He would never have to observe another atomic bomb. Medically, mostly thanks to you and his godfather he is excluded from that kind of duty and he is back to normal, mentally and physically.'

'The dread is there that he might have trouble. When you go shopping, make an early start before he goes to lunch with the brass hats. I am going to give him a session of hypnosis again, just to reassure him.'

'No wonder he wants you to join them in America.'

'They want both of us but they ought to go home, Emma. I've noticed how easy it is for Bea to depend on you again and Dwight must never have a tame shrink at his elbow full time. It isn't healthy. I deplore the growing trend in the States for people to have a regular session on the couch just as routine as a hair-do.'

'Bea depend on *me?*' She found it amusing. 'She was always a source of strength to me, not the other way round.'

Paul slipped into bed and held her slightly thickening body with care and adoration. 'Silly girl. Bea can be completely relaxed with you as you've shared so much. She could never say such outrageous things to the more buttoned-up Ivy League types with whom she has to mix and socialise, nor to the ones at the other end of the scale who would try to take advantage if she made them feel too relaxed and wanted. It's a fine line Emma. We talk of

English snobbery, but the demarcations of society over there are just as rigid but under the surface and can be misunderstood. She misses you and will never have a friend she loves more. Believe it or not, over the years you have influenced her as much as she has done for you and it will be so whenever she thinks of you. Dwight needs to be with his own people, confident with his family and his war record but preferably on the ranch, his own domain.'

'You think that Dwight is weak?'

'Less strong than Bea,' he said gently. 'He has his own strengths and they are very happy but Bea is the one who will hold that family together, and she will make any sacrifice to do so, but she will need to cling to us for solid comfort and must know that we are here.'

Sleepily, Emma snuggled close. 'Tomorrow I must buy some rubber ducks for the twins' baths.'

'What brought that on?'

'I can't see them coming to visit the real ones in St James's Park until they are older but Bea can tell them all about the real ducks in the park.'

'Don't promise them the zoo! Ducks will be enough.'

Emma giggled. 'No elephants.'

Paul listened to her regular breathing and drew his arm away as it was having pins and needles. Emma stirred and wriggled closer. He placed a hand on her taut abdomen and smiled. Hope and unbelievable happiness flooded over him as he felt the tiny movements and knew his child was there, waiting.

## Chapter Sixteen

'I suppose that MacArthur's oratory swung the opinions of the top brass,' Dwight said. 'I believe that the Chief of Naval Staff was almost in tears when he agreed to the invasion of Inchon. Many were afraid that what Churchill said about the Anzio landings might happen again. You recall?'

'Not vividly but I'm sure you've read it up.' Paul sounded patient and amused. Dwight had discovered war history in a big way and now that he was safely back in America he could view the scene in Korea with detachment and with the interest of a budding historian, and—as all converts to a creed—was more enthusiastic than the people who had grown up with history all round them.

'Churchill said at that time that such an invasion was "Not a wild cat to tear out the heart of the Boche, but a stranded whale". Well, our whale swam and we made the long walk and over the Han river with Mac riding high on a motorcade, would you believe it, on a specially constructed bridge?'

'We *did* want to know how Bea is,' Paul pointed out gently.

'Bea's fine and the twins are ready for their new brother or sister, and of course, Yuletide.'

Bea's voice came through over the phone. 'Go and feed the chickens,' she said crossly. 'No, not you, Paul. I think my husband has finally flipped. He reads books! Not girlie magazines; real books, and then tells me all about wars in Europe, wars in India and wars wherever he can find them. It will be toy soldiers next,' she added in a low voice. 'Battle games for the retired service man.'

'I thought the main interest was genealogy?'

Bea sighed. 'He was on the trail of an

300

ancestor who fought for the Yanks after the Boston tea party, but he had to admit his sympathies were not with him as he had a nasty reputation over slavery.'

'In the North?'

'A lot of absentee owners of cotton fields lived in the North. I thought you wanted to know if I was having twinges. You are as bad as Dwight. What about *me?*'

'I'll pass you over to Emma. You sound like a very healthy, expectant mother, Bea, and Dwight sounded fine too. I wanted a word with him and I can tell that he is OK. Good luck and we send all our best love.'

'Emma? How is my fat friend?' Bea asked with a complete lack of feeling for a fellow sufferer.

'Fat,' Emma agreed.

'You will ring me every day after the baby is born? I feel as if they have turned me over to a bunch of foreigners and I'll need to hear your voice.'

'Foreigners? They are your chosen people, the countrymen and women of your husband's forefathers.'

'The last time I was being delivered I was in Beatties where everyone spoke intelligible English, not a hint of Bronx or

Southern Belle or a bit of Spanish thrown in. Do you know the nurses never wear black stockings—they have white dresses, white shoes and caps and pale stockings. I feel as if I am surrounded by ghosts.'

'In fact you are enjoying life. That old caustic wit has not deserted you.'

'I long to hear a cockney bus driver call me *luv* and I have a passion for apple pie as Emily makes it.'

'When did you ever ride on a London bus since we trained at Beatties?'

'Don't spoil it. I want a good wallow about the old days.'

'Look at your photo album and check over your clothes, as you sound very restless. Is it going to happen today?'

'Soon, they say. I shall go in tomorrow and be waited on by an army of crisp toothpaste-smile girls who will be briskly impersonal and spend the time talking about boyfriends and films at the central desk outside the room where I shall pant and heave and be temperamental.'

'Think of it as one golden thread in life's bright tapestry, as Sister Foster used to say.'

'I'll repeat that to you when your time comes, smarty-pants.'

'I'll be in touch. Dwight promised to let us know what progress you make and we shall be here waiting.'

'Bless you.'

Emma heard a sob and the line went dead. 'She's frightened.'

Paul nodded. 'Dwight said as much but is it surprising at this stage? You are here, so many miles away and even her father and Miranda are out of reach. She'll be fine, Emma. In a way I wish that you were not having our baby soon after her. Her fear might rub off.'

'Apart from missing Bea I have everything I want now.' She laughed. 'I have almost too much attention. Mrs Coster pops her head round the kitchen door at least once an hour to see if I'm still there. Eileen has been marvellous, and I'm not due yet.'

'Let's enjoy a quiet Christmas on our own. Last Christmas was wonderful, with lots of friends staying with us, but we don't need a lot of extra people here now, do we?'

'I'll go up and see the nursery. It still smells of distemper but it's getting better and as there's no wind today I'll open the windows.'

The room was clean and bright with pale yellow curtains and a chartreuse day bed in one corner. The Turkish rugs and walnut furniture took away the clinical austerity of the trolley already laid up with bowls, a bucket and a pile of clean nappies put discreetly behind the screen that would keep any draughts from the papier-mâche baby bath on the stand.

Emma opened the door of the large linen cupboard. The workmen had wanted to re-paper it inside as the paper was faded but she had refused and had locked the door until the rest of the room was finished.

Emma looked beyond the clean linen and saw the frieze of painted animals. She pushed a large sachet of lavender between the towels and her eyes were misty.

I knew I must keep this room for my own baby, she thought. If there's a trace of the children who lived in this room they have left a gentle presence, not ghosts but a good loving influence. I shall keep lavender in here for my baby.

Eileen asked if it was really all right if she went to the pictures with Mick. 'Make the most of me now,' Emma said. 'I'll give the six o'clock feed and you will be back for the last one. Has Mick booked for the pantomime? You are to go! I've arranged for a friend to stay for two days who can cope with a small baby if I don't feel up to it. It will give both of us a rest and I'll enjoy her company. We haven't invited any more people, so you must take time for yourselves now.'

The waiting hung over her like a hovering cloud, not a rain cloud, but pink round the edges. Emma knew now how Bea was feeling. Emily Darwen rang only to ask about Bea as if Emma's event would be at a far distant time.

The telephone rang now and Paul answered it while Emma mixed the six o'clock feed for baby Jean. 'Guess what?' he asked laconically.

'Aunt Emily again?' Emma pushed the bottle teat into the willing mouth and the baby began to suck.

'Two down and one to go.' Paul laughed with sheer pleasure.

'Bea? But I was speaking to her a few hours ago!'

'She had started labour then but thought it was indigestion and it was quick. One fine boy delivered and as they say, mother and child doing well. Dwight had to ring his parents so there was no time for details but he'll fill us in tomorrow.'

Jean burped when the feed was over and Emma put her back in the cot. 'I don't think she's dirty so I'll try to get Aunt Emily now before I change her.'

'Too late.' Paul handed her the receiver. 'I left it to you to tell her. *Now*, I may be able to get on with some work!'

'Bea had a boy,' Emma announced with no preamble. 'So now she has two boys and a girl.'

'I'm glad that's over.' Emily sounded very relieved.

'You didn't sense anything wrong, did you?'

'Not really, so long as his breathing is all right.'

'Dwight told Paul that the baby was bawling loud and clear, so his lungs must be fine.'

'Good. How are you with all this excitement?'

'A little sad as I am far away from her and she is a bit lonely. Dwight promised to be in touch later. Poor man. He is probably sleeping now but it will be day soon over there and we'll hear from him at ten or after, so no bed until he rings.'

'I'm going over to Janey for Christmas

but I shall be back when you have your baby. She won't be ready to be born at Christmas.'

'I've always felt sorry for people who have Christmas and birthday at the same time. They lose a lot of excitement and have fewer presents.'

Paul added his greetings and when they were back in the kitchen making bedtime drinks and waiting for the call from America, Paul was pensive. 'I wish we could persuade Emily to visit us here. Aunt Janey is in Hampshire and the worst of the journey there is the crossing by ferry if the sea is rough. A car journey after that would not be difficult or trying and I think that your baby will mean a lot to her.'

'We'll insist that she comes here in the spring. Dr Sutton has tried to bring her here when he comes up for medical conferences and the last time he asked her she nearly said yes, so maybe he can bring her to us. They could both stay here, as he is interested in your work.'

Emma started up when the phone rang. Dwight sounded tired but jubilant. 'She's fine and he's fine, but I don't know about me. I feel bushed.'

'Everything went well? No panics?'

'He chose his words carefully as if she might be alarmed. 'All well now after they got his airway clear. He had a build up of mucus in his tubes and was a touch blue but they soon got him yelling.'

'Is that all?'

'That's it. Why, did Emily expect a crisis?'

'Just his breathing,' Emma admitted.

'Never let her come near Salem! Even now they look sideways at witches. Bea will be in touch as soon as she's had a long sleep. Happy Christmas.'

'This year, I'll be glad when it's over. Give our love to Bea and ... what do you call him?'

'Another family name that Bea will never use unless he robs a bank, so for her he's Mark and for my folks Arnold.'

'I do see her point.'

'We could call him Arnie.'

'Forget it.' Emma laughed, 'Give our love to Mark.'

'Mark?' Paul tried it out and smiled. 'I like it. Have you decided what we'll call ours?'

'You haven't been a lot of help and each time I think of a name I am not convinced that it is the right one. There are old superstitions that say it's unlucky to be sure about a name until the baby is born. I think it's because no baby looks like anyone but Winston Churchill for the first day or so and might not live up to the chosen name. Some shops selling prams hold on to what has been ordered until after the birth, with a guarantee that they will not hold the parents to any purchase that is not needed.' Her lip trembled.

'Sensible, but macabre.' Paul sounded disapproving.

She took a deep breath. 'I have faith in Aunt Emily and the way I feel now. Don't look so worried Paul. I'm fine and now that Bea is over hers I can slide lazily into a kind of rosy anticipation, something new that I have never experienced.'

'You have enough baby clothes for three, so with any luck you can tactfully refuse any of Jean's that she outgrows. Eileen is a gem but she has peculiar tastes and I wouldn't want a child of ours in mauve tops and yellow pants.'

'I think she wishes she'd called the baby Pansy, hence the fixation with mauve! Mick is quite firm about it and Jean it will be as far as he is concerned when she is christened.'

Each morning, Emma felt the movements in her womb, and each day she grew heavier in body. But not in her mood; she had time to think about Paul and Bea and Emily and some of the past with love, but she knew with a strange detachment that she wanted none of them with her when the baby was delivered.

Bea, when she was expecting the twins had insisted that she needed no person other than the professionals with her while she laboured. Birth, the ancient life force was a private affair, a primitive ceremony for women.

Christmas came and went almost unnoticed except for the carollers and the decorated fir tree that Eileen and Mick went to see in Trafalgar Square, a present from Norway in gratitude for help during the war. The hoped for white Christmas didn't appear and the damp, mild days lingered.

'Twice you've said that you hope the weather stays like this,' Emma remarked. 'I wish we could have a breeze and a frost to clear the air. At night I find it stifling.'

Paul said nothing but she noticed that

he had fewer names in the casebook than he had over the Christmas and New Year period, but used the telephone more often.

Mick left the house only when Paul was in the office, as if someone must stay in charge, and during one early morning when Emma felt the first twinge, Mick disappeared.

Paul alerted Stella Morgan who advised admission to the private wing of Beatties and a small ambulance car arrived to collect her and Paul.

As they drove through the empty dawn streets she turned to him. 'Why this one? Is your car out of order?' she asked without real curiosity as the contractions were increasing in tone and regularity. 'How will you get back?'

'There are such things as cabs.'

'Mick could collect you.'

'Sister Sykes, this is no time to try to organise us. You have work to do!'

The room was pretty but spare, as if ready for anything, and Emma was glad to slide between the sheets while a nurse unpacked the small overnight bag. 'Do you want me to stay?' Paul asked.

'No, Darling. Go home until it's over.'

Another contraction built up and passed. 'As you can see I have no time for small talk,' she added when her breath returned to normal. 'Just leave me my watch so that I can time them.'

'She has a fairly long way to go,' Stella said later, after Emma had been examined and when he found Stella in the office. 'We'll give her a rest later and then stimulate her when she has to start pushing.'

'I should be used to hospitals,' he said ruefully. 'I feel like a complete beginner, as if all my experience is for nothing.'

'Babies are different.' Stella gave a broad smile. 'It gives me pleasure to see strong men in this state. It means they care.'

'I care,' he said with feeling. 'But may I go home now? I'll be in later.'

He decided to walk some of the way home and stopped for a late luncheon snack, but as the rain began to fall he hailed a taxi.

His car was at the door of the house and he paid off the taxi and hurried inside and upstairs. Voices in the kitchen led him there. 'This is wonderful. Quite frankly, I never thought it possible.'

He caught Emily Darwen in a firm

embrace and for once she didn't back away from the wave of affection.

'I'm having a cup of tea,' she announced. 'That young man has all the right ideas. Who told him I like a nip of whisky in it? He made it as strong as I like it. How is Emma?'

'Fine. Everything is going well.'

'I'll get unpacked now.'

'I'll take you up when you've finished your tea. It's so good to see you, Emily. I hope you aren't tired.'

'No, it was easy. I was all ready to start out on the first ferry, and Mick drove fast, but very well. He's the one who should be tired, doing the journey twice in one day. I can stay for three days then I have to get back. Dr Sutton will take me back if you tell him I'm here, as he will be coming to London tomorrow to meet people.'

'He rang and he'll be ready to take you back. He's anxious to see my clinic so I invited him to stay.'

'Everything is working out.' Emily looked as pleased as if she had planned the whole event. 'I cooked a gammon joint and brought it, and Dr Sutton said he'd bring something when he comes.' She looked round the kitchen. 'Is there a cold larder?'

'The ham can go in the fridge.'

She pointed. 'That is the ham but I need somewhere cool and not frosty for this.' She unwrapped a shoebox from its thick newspaper cover and took it to the larder. 'Something for Emma,' she remarked in a way that discouraged questions.

At midnight, Paul contacted Stella Morgan. She sounded busy. 'Come in at one.'

'I'll drive you, Guv,' Mick said. 'You did the same for me and I know what a state I was in! I'll do it,' he insisted. 'I had a kip this evening in case you needed me and I'm fresh as a daisy.'

Emily sat back in a deep armchair. 'I'll have the kettle on when I hear the car come back,' she promised and Paul didn't suggest that she went to bed.

Stella Morgan looked tired. 'Sister will tell you all about it but I must get to bed as I have a ward round at eight tomorrow. Congratulations Paul, you have a lovely daughter. Emma's back in her room and the baby is being cleaned up.'

Paul sat down heavily on the seat by the door of Emma's room and Mick grinned. 'I know the feeling. I'll be downstairs waiting. They won't let you stay for long the first time. She'll need her sleep.' He grinned with the superiority of a man who knew the ropes from personal experience. 'Glad it's a girl. They are better behaved than boys.'

Paul laughed and relaxed. 'I thought you wanted train sets?'

'Na! Get in and see your missus.'

Emma was pale and limp but she held out her arms to Paul and he embraced her gently. She smiled. 'She's beautiful. I wanted to be alone to have her but now I need to show her off to the world.'

Her eyelids drooped and after ten minutes, Paul crept away. He saw the bundle of white towelling that held his red-faced daughter, in the arms of the nurse by the window at the nursery entrance, and was filled with peace. Tomorrow Emma would be strong enough for one other visitor and he might be allowed to hold his daughter.

Emily was bright-eyed and made strong tea for her and Mick and cocoa for Paul. 'You knew it would be a girl.' Mick eyed her with respect. 'Crikey, we could do with you here in the clinic.'

'She works in one on the Island and

tomorrow you will meet the doctor who thinks he runs it.'

'Did you tell Emma I was here?'

'You said not to, and I obeyed. You can go in tomorrow and take that shoebox with you. I thought you'd sorted out Emma's memorabilia and I can't think what you need to keep cool,' Paul teased her.

'I filled my hot water bottle and I'm going to bed. If I'd known it was so comfortable here I'd have been here before now.'

Emily clutched the box all the way to Beatties and after Paul had warned Emma that Emily had made the dreaded journey to see her, she was shown into the room.

'Well now, my girl! You are a mother now.' Emily gave her a self-conscious hug but smiled as if her face would crack, and after a few minutes Emma looked at the shoebox with ill-concealed curiosity.

'A present for the baby?'

'Don't ask me. I was not allowed to see it,' Paul asserted.

Emily blushed. 'It seemed a good idea when I picked them at three in the morning, but you might like them.'

Emma took off the lid and gasped. On a bed of damp green moss lay five blossoms.

The waxy cream petals backed pale yellow stamens and a scent of spring came as the box was opened. No leaves, just the delicate flowers and pale green calyxes.

'Your Christmas rose.' Emma's eyes filled with tears. 'You told me once of your brother's wife, who was sweet and delicate and was named Rose.' She looked at Paul and he nodded happily. 'We'll call the baby Rosamund for best—but for everyday, she'll be just Rose.'

The publishers hope that this book has given you enjoyable reading. Large Print Books are especially designed to be as easy to see and hold as possible. If you wish a complete list of our books, please ask at your local library or write directly to: Magna Large Print Books, Long Preston, North Yorkshire, BD23 4ND, England.